Alison Moore's short sto
British Short Stories, Best
Horror, and broadcast on
her first collection, *The Pr*
won the New Writer Nove ... Her first novel, *The Lighthouse*, was shortlisted for the Man Booker Prize and the National Book Awards (New Writer of the Year), winning the McKitterick Prize. Both *The Lighthouse* and her second novel, *He Wants*, were Observer Books of the Year. She recently published her fifth novel, *The Retreat*, and a trilogy for children, beginning with *Sunny and the Ghosts*. Born in Manchester in 1971, she lives in a village on the Leicestershire-Nottinghamshire border with her husband Dan and son Arthur, and is an honorary lecturer in the School of English at the University of Nottingham.

ALSO BY ALISON MOORE

NOVELS

The Lighthouse (2012)

He Wants (2014)

Death and the Seaside (2016)

Missing (2018)

The Retreat (2021)

SHORT STORIES

The Pre-War House and Other Stories (2013)

CHILDREN'S FICTION

Sunny and the Ghosts (2018)

Sunny and the Hotel Splendid (2019)

Sunny and the Wicked Lady (2020)

ALISON MOORE

EASTMOUTH

AND OTHER STORIES

SALT
MODERN
STORIES

CROMER

PUBLISHED BY SALT PUBLISHING 2022

2 4 6 8 10 9 7 5 3 1

First published in Great Britain in 2022 by
Salt Publishing Ltd
12 Norwich Road, Cromer, Norfolk NR27 0AX United Kingdom

www.saltpublishing.com

Salt Publishing Limited Reg. No. 5293401

A CIP catalogue record for this book is available from the British Library

ISBN 978 1 78463 274 8 (Paperback edition)
ISBN 978 1 78463 275 5 (Electronic edition)

Typeset in Granjon by Salt Publishing

Printed and bound in Great Britain by Clays Ltd, St Ives plc

For Isabel and Sue

Contents

Eastmouth

SONIA STANDS ON the slabs of the promenade, looking out across the pebbly beach. It is like so many of the seaside resorts from her childhood. She remembers one whose tarred pebbles left their sticky blackness on her bare feet and legs and the seat of her swimsuit. She had to be scrubbed red raw in the bath at the B&B. Her hands are wrapped around the railings, whose old paint is flaking off. When she lets go, her palms will smell of rust.

The visibility is poor. She can't see land beyond Eastmouth.

'I've missed the sound of the gulls,' says Peter, watching them circling overhead.

He says this, thinks Sonia, as if he has not heard them for years, but during the time they've been at university, he got the train home most weekends. Sonia does not think she would have missed the gulls. She is used to the Midlands and to city life.

She lets go of the railings and they walk on down the promenade. Sonia, in a thin, brightly coloured jacket, has dressed for warmer weather. Shivering, she huddles into herself. 'Let's get you home,' says Peter. For the last half hour of their journey, while the train was pulling in and all the way from the station he's been saying things like that: 'We're almost home,' and, 'Won't it be nice to be home?' as if this were her home too. Their suitcases, pulled on wheels behind them, are noisy on the crooked slabs. 'They'll know we're here,' says Peter.

'Who will?' asks Sonia.

'Everyone,' says Peter.

Sonia, looking around, sees a lone figure in the bay window of a retirement home, and a woman in a transparent mac sitting on a bench in a shelter. Peter nods at the woman as they pass.

'It's quiet,' says Sonia.

'It's quiet most of the year,' says Peter.

He points out a modernist, pre-war building just ahead of them. 'I've always loved coming to see the shows,' he says. 'My all-time favourite act is Cannon and Ball.' Reaching this seafront pavilion, they stop to look at the posters. 'Look,' says Peter, 'Cannon and Ball.' He is beaming, cheerful when he says, 'Nothing changes.'

Peter lets them into the house with a key that he wears on a chain around his neck. His mother comes into the hallway with her arms wide open, saying to Sonia as much as to Peter, 'You're home!' Taking Sonia's jacket, looking at its bright colours, she says to Sonia, 'Blue and green should never be seen!' and then she puts the jacket away.

As they sit down to dinner, Peter's mother says, 'Sonia, what were you planning to do with your summer?'

'I've applied for a job up north,' says Sonia. 'I had the

interview yesterday, and I think it went well. I should hear tomorrow whether or not I've got it. I gave them this number – Peter said that was all right. If I get the job, I'll save up for a while and then I want to go to Las Vegas.' She mentions pictures she's seen of the place, all the lights.

'If you like that sort of thing,' says Peter's father, 'you should take an evening stroll along our prom. You'll see it all lit up.' He chews his food for a while before saying, 'It's a lot hotter there, though. It wouldn't suit me. We stick to England, the south coast.'

A gust rattles the window and Sonia turns to see the wind stripping the last of the leaves from a potted shrub in the back yard.

'Look,' says Peter's father, 'the sun's coming out for you,' and he nods towards a patch of sunlight the colour of weak urine on a whitewashed, breeze-block wall.

Peter's mother opens the wine and says to Sonia, 'You'll be needing this.' Sonia supposes she is referring to their long train journey, or perhaps the cold weather; it isn't clear.

'It's nice to have you home,' says Peter's mother, later, when they are clearing the table.

'I think Peter's glad to be home,' says Sonia.

'And what about you?'

'I don't live here,' says Sonia. She is surprised that Peter's mother does not know this.

'You didn't grow up here,' agrees Peter's mother. Opening the back door, she throws the scraps into the yard and the seagulls appear out of nowhere, descending instantly, filling the yard with their shrieks. 'Our home is your home,' she says, as she closes the door, 'but I do remember what it's like to be young and independent. There are lots of empty flats around here and they always need people at the pavilion. The place is crying out for young blood.'

'I wasn't planning on staying long,' says Sonia.

Peter's mother nods. She looks around the kitchen and says, 'Well, I think that will do. I'll go and change the sheets on your bed.'

Their bags are side by side in the corner of Peter's bedroom. Hers has a sticker on the side saying *I ♥ Las Vegas*, even though she has never been there. His has a label giving his name – Peter Webster – and his home address, his parents' address, so that it can't get lost.

They go to bed early but Sonia lies awake in the darkness, in between the cold wall and Peter, who is fast asleep. She finally drops off in the early hours before being woken at dawn by what she thinks is the sound of babies crying, but it is only the gulls.

Sonia, in the bathroom, doing up the belt of her jeans, can hear Peter's mother talking on the phone at the bottom of the stairs. 'No,' she is saying, 'I don't want it. I've changed my mind. Please don't call here again.' Sonia checks her face in the mirror before coming out, finding Peter's mother on the landing now, outside the bathroom door. 'All right, dear?' says Peter's mother. 'Come down to breakfast. I've made pancakes with syrup, just like they have in America!'

Sonia stays in all day. At the end of the afternoon, at ten to five, she phones the company she had hoped would call to offer her a job. She speaks to a receptionist who says, 'Please hold.' Then she speaks to a secretary who tells her that the job has been offered to someone else. The secretary sounds impatient and terminates the conversation as soon as she can. Sonia redials – she has some questions to ask – but no one picks up; they've all gone home.

When Sonia goes up to bed that night, she finds that the sticker on her bag has been doctored with a permanent marker. 'Las' has been neatly changed to 'East' but 'Vegas' required a heavier hand, a thicker line. *I ♥ Eastmouth.*

The following day is Saturday. After breakfast, Sonia watches the dead-eyed gulls gathering on the wall of the yard. They grab at the scraps Peter's mother puts out, and if the door is not kept closed they will come inside, wanting the cat food, taking more than they have been given.

'I think I'll go for a walk,' says Sonia.

'I'll come with you,' says Peter, beginning to get to his feet.

'I'd rather go on my own,' says Sonia. Mr and Mrs Webster stop what they are doing and look at her. They watch her as she leaves the room.

She puts on her shoes and looks for her jacket but she can't find it. She asks Peter's mother if she's seen it and Peter's mother says, 'I'm washing it. Wear mine.' She takes down a heavy beige coat and helps Sonia into it. 'Yours was too thin anyway,' says Peter's mother. 'You'll need something warmer now you're here.'

Sonia walks a mile along the promenade before coming to a stop, leaning on the railings and looking out to sea, watching a yellow helicopter that is circling in the distance. As a child, she used to wave to rescue helicopters even though she knew they weren't really looking for her; she just did it for fun or for practice. She raises her hands now and waves, scissoring her arms above her head, like semaphore, as if she were someone in a high-vis jacket on a runway, although she does not know semaphore; she does not know how to say 'stop'. The helicopter turns away and leaves.

'Sonia.'

She turns around and finds Peter's parents standing behind her.

'We thought we'd walk with you,' says Peter's mother. 'What a good idea, a little leg stretch.'

They walk along with her, nodding to the woman in the transparent mac as they pass the shelter.

When they reach the end of the promenade, Peter's father says, 'We should turn back,' and as they walk Sonia home again they tell her about the evening's entertainment: a show at the pavilion and dinner at the Grand.

'I've booked you a table,' says Peter's father. 'It's a fine place. It's where I proposed to Peter's mother. We go there every year for our anniversary.'

'Have the seafood platter,' says Peter's mother.

Peter, wearing one of his father's ties, walks Sonia along the blustery promenade. The seafront is all lit up with lightbulbs strung between the lampposts. 'See?' says Peter. 'Who needs Las Vegas?' At the pavilion, they see an Elvis, who, like his thin costume, looks tired. When the show is over, they go on to the Grand.

They are greeted as 'Mr and Mrs Webster' and Sonia opens her mouth to correct the misapprehension but they are already being led through the restaurant towards their table in the corner, and in the end she says nothing.

7

When the waiter comes to take their order, Sonia asks for a pasta dish.

'Are you not going to have the seafood platter?' asks Peter.

'I don't think so,' says Sonia.

Peter looks concerned. He orders his own meal without looking at the menu.

Sonia, looking around at the decor, says to Peter, 'I doubt they've changed a thing since your parents first came here.'

Peter touches the flock wallpaper and says, 'That's a nice thought.'

The waiter returns to light their candle and pour the wine. They raise their glasses, touching the thin rims together. Sonia brings hers close to her mouth but barely wets her lips before putting it down again.

'All right?' says Peter.

Sonia nods. She has not yet told him about the test she did in his parents' bathroom, about the white plastic stick with the little window in the middle, the vertical line that proved the test was working, and the sky-blue, sea-blue flat line that made her think of a distant horizon seen through an aeroplane window. She has not told him that when she came out of the bathroom with the plastic stick still in her hand, Peter's mother was standing there, and that when, after breakfast, she looked for the stick, it had been moved.

The waiter returns with their meals. Peter, smiling down at the food on his plate, picking up his fork, begins to talk to Sonia about the possibility of a management position at the pavilion. His dad, he says, can pull a few strings.

The waiter is coming back already. He is going to ask them if everything is all right, and Sonia is going to say yes even though she has barely had a taste yet. Peter is holding his fork out across the table towards Sonia, offering her a piece of something whose fishy smell reminds her of the stony beach, the tarry pebbles, and the gulls that will wake her at dawn.

She sees, in the molten wax around the wick of the candle, an insect. Sonia picks up her fork, aiming the handle into this hot moat. She is an air-sea rescue unit arriving on the scene to lift the insect to safety. Carefully, she places the insect on a serviette to recover, as if it has only been floating in a sticky drink.

'I think that one's had it,' says Peter, and Sonia looks at it and has to agree.

Peter, who had the whole bottle of wine to himself, is still sleeping the next morning when Sonia gets up, puts on the beige coat and lets herself out of the house. She walks down the promenade again, away from Peter's parents' house, heading in the direction she and Peter came from when they arrived here. She goes as far as the end of the promenade, where she stops to watch the gulls, and then she goes further, climbing up above the town until she is standing a hundred metres above sea level in the wind. She is still in Eastmouth, though. She cannot see across to the next town. When she looks at her watch, she realises that she has been gone for a while now. As she makes her way down from the cliffs, she hears the tolling of a bell; it is coming from the church that stands on top of one of the hills that surround the otherwise flat town.

On the promenade, all the shelters are empty. All the bay windows of all the retirement homes are empty. She realises that it's Sunday and wonders if everyone's at church.

Peter's parents might be there, and perhaps even Peter.

She veers slightly away from the promenade now. It is the start of the summer and ought to be warmer, but it is windy and cold and she is glad of Peter's mother's coat. She has her purse in the pocket. She heads down a side street that brings her out at the train station, which is overlooked by the church.

Alone on the platform, she stands in front of the train timetable. She looks at her watch, although pointlessly, as it turns out, because when she consults the timetable she finds that no trains run on Sundays. She wanders to the edge of the platform and looks along the tracks in the direction she would go to get home, and then in the opposite direction. Is there really nothing at all on a Sunday, she wonders, does nothing even pass through?

She is still there when she notices that the woman in the transparent mac is now standing at one end of the platform. She is talking on a mobile phone but she is looking at Sonia and so Sonia nods at her. She doesn't know whether she has been recognised. The woman, putting away the phone, approaches. When she is within touching distance, she says, 'You're the Websters' girl.'

'No,' says Sonia, preparing to introduce herself, whilst at the same time noticing the locals coming down the hill, coming from church. The service is over. It seems as if the whole town is heading towards them, like an army in beige and lilac.

'Yes,' says the woman. 'You are. You're the Websters' girl.'

The crowd is nearing the foot of the hill; they are close now and one by one they look at the woman in the transparent mac and they nod.

May Day

His tyres rumbled for hours down grey roads that went on and on, year after year. It became soporific. The journey ended in the car park beneath the Parisian street on which his ex-wife and daughter now lived. He locked the car and walked to Lionel's flat, where he rang the doorbell and waited.

Lionel came to the door, smelling of his Gauloises cigarettes. 'Gareth,' he said. He made it sound like 'garret,' like somewhere lonely and draughty. When Gareth had to say Lionel's name, he said it the English way. Caroline always said it the French way, and Gareth could tell that she enjoyed the feel of the word in her mouth. 'Have you had a good journey?' he asked.

'Not too bad,' said Gareth, coming into the hallway with his weekend bag and a bottle of coffee liqueur, a gift, which Lionel took. They went into the kitchen, where Caroline air-kissed Gareth with a paring knife in her hand.

'Rebecca will be home soon,' said Lionel, 'and dinner's on the way. Come with me.'

He led Gareth into the living room, offering him an armchair and taking for himself a place on the two-seater sofa, next to Caroline's knitting. Lionel lit up a cigarette and offered one to Gareth. Gareth held up his hands in refusal. He must look, he thought, like a man surrendering. 'I'll take a drink, though,' he said.

Lionel blew smoke out of his nostrils. He got up and went to a drinks cabinet in the corner of the room. Gareth could not imagine how they managed always to keep it stocked, when he himself was unable to open a bottle of whisky without finishing it before bedtime.

'Same as usual?' asked Lionel.

Gareth nodded. He watched the whisky being poured; he did not need it watered down as Lionel did, or mixed with Caroline's ginger ale. The glass was in his hand when he heard the door to the flat open and close. He heard an exchange in the hallway between Caroline and his daughter, and after a while Rebecca sloped into view. She looked so tall, this long-limbed, long-haired girl; she looked like a teenager, which at twelve she nearly was. He must not tell her that she had grown; she hated that.

'Hi, Dad,' she said, coming into the living room.

'Rebecca,' said Lionel, beckoning her over to where he sat. They exchanged a greeting that was part embrace and part kiss, and Gareth found it hard to watch. It was one of the first things that he had noticed about Lionel: how *tactile* he was.

Rebecca turned to Gareth, who put his glass down empty on a side table. It had been so easy to cuddle her when she was little, but at some point that had stopped. She approached, kissed the space on either side of him, and moved away again. Tomorrow, the two of them would get out of Lionel's flat, where it was impossible to relax; he and Rebecca would have all day together, without Lionel always being there. He imagined them walking arm in arm beside the Seine, and sitting in a café; he would buy a bottle of Burgundy and give Rebecca her first taste of wine.

'I wanted to go to the catacombs,' said Rebecca.

Gareth bowed his head. 'I know,' he said. It had been his idea in the first place, to explore the city's subterranean ossuaries. Foolishly, he had made his daughter a promise that he now found he could not keep. 'The thing is, it turns out, it's closed on Sunday and Monday, and I have to drive home on Tuesday. I have to get back to work.'

'You said it was open on Sunday,' said Rebecca.

'Yes,' said Gareth, 'it normally is, but not on the first of May.' The information was right there on the website, but he had not seen it, or had not understood; it was all in French.

'So the two days you're here, it's closed,' said Rebecca.

'I'm sorry,' said Gareth, 'but we'll do something else.'

Rebecca rolled her eyes.

'You can see a video of the catacombs on the Internet,' he said. He had seen it; he had seen the walls of skulls.

'That's hardly the same,' said Rebecca.

'I know,' said Gareth.

'What *are* we going to do tomorrow, then?' asked Rebecca.

'Well,' said Gareth, 'I thought we could go down the sewers.'

'The *sewers*?'

'Yes,' said Gareth. 'The sewer system is a network of underground tunnels, just like the catacombs, but the sewers are even older.'

'And they stink,' said Rebecca.

Caroline called from the kitchen, 'Rebecca, go and wash your hands before dinner.'

Rebecca made a face but Lionel said, 'Now, Rebecca,' and Rebecca went to wash her hands.

'Please excuse me,' said Lionel. He left the room, turning towards the kitchen, where Gareth imagined him putting his hands on Caroline, speaking to her in French, and she would understand him, smile at him, give him something to carry.

Gareth took his glass over to the drinks cabinet and poured himself a generous measure.

Lionel stood at the head of the table, carving the meat while everyone watched. Caroline had put on some music, much of which Gareth did not recognise, and what he did recognise he did not remember her ever having listened to before. The Bee Gees came on, and Caroline said that her favourite was Barry Gibb, and that she had always preferred him with a beard. 'I do like a man with a beard,' she said, and Lionel stroked his goatee.

A bottle of red wine was already open on the table, and Lionel poured out three glasses. He raised his – 'To family . . .' – and they drank, and then Lionel passed his glass to Rebecca so that she could have a taste. He turned to Gareth and asked, 'Are you still scuba-diving?'

Gareth said that he was.

'But only in the Thames,' said Lionel.

'I like the Thames,' said Gareth.

Caroline used to say to him, after a Thames Estuary dive, 'You smell of the river.' She meant it in a bad way but Gareth loved the river and was addicted to its cold briny tang.

He detailed his most recent wreck dive and told the story about Henry IV's coffin, which was on its way down the Thames to Canterbury Cathedral when a storm broke and the body was thrown overboard.

'You told this story before,' said Lionel. 'I don't think it's true.'

'Whether he's under the Thames or sealed in a tomb, he's dead either way,' said Rebecca.

Most of Gareth's dives had been under thirty metres, but recently he had started going deeper. There was a table in his diving manual that showed the effects of nitrogen narcosis on the diver, which began as soon as the diver started his descent and which increased with depth. Even at twenty metres, the diver had mildly impaired reasoning. The diver did not notice it himself. Or perhaps he was aware of something like a softening of the senses. It was restful down there. At thirty metres, the diver began to make errors of calculation, and below fifty metres, euphoria could turn into hysterical laughter and terror, before giving way to hallucinations. Well, he had never been that far down, but he had got down to forty-two metres. You had to keep your eye on your depth gauge or the temptation was to keep going deeper.

'I would not like it,' said Lionel. 'I would feel claustrophobic, in that mask you have to wear, and with all those tonnes of water on top of you, and it must get dark down there.'

'It does,' said Gareth. He had been on dives where it was hard to see anything except for the blackness of the water itself. It was disorienting. You could feel disconnected; you could feel peaceful. It was essentially sensory deprivation, as used in both therapy and torture.

'We prefer tennis,' said Lionel, throwing a smile in Caroline's direction. 'It keeps us young.'

Gareth ran a hand over his head, over the inches where his hair used to be. He felt like a monk.

'Who is caring for your dog while you are here?' asked Lionel.

'He died,' said Gareth. 'He had a tumour.'

'He *died*?' said Rebecca.

'You can't just announce something like that,' said Caroline, 'over the dinner table with no warning.'

Rebecca was crying.

'It's surprising, actually,' said Gareth, 'what can be announced over the dinner table with no warning.' He reached for the wine bottle, refilled his glass and ate in silence while Caroline comforted their daughter.

He woke feeling anxious, with a racing heart and clammy skin. He felt as if his brain had shrunk; deep within the walls of his skull, he could feel it pulsing.

He was on the short sofa, in a sleeping bag. The curtains were closed but there were gaps through which he could see daylight.

His wine glass was still there on a side table. He raised himself up on his elbows, picked up his glass and drained the dregs.

He lay down again, wanting to go back to sleep. He tried to get comfortable on Lionel's sofa but was unable to make himself fit. He kept sliding off.

His bladder eventually forced him to get up. He unzipped his sleeping bag and made his way into the hallway. Across from the living room, through an open door, he could see the master bedroom, which reeked of Lionel's Gauloises. He saw the dishevelled bed.

In the bathroom, Gareth pissed and showered but did not shave. He emerged just as Caroline was leaving for work. Standing in the hallway with her coat already on, she looked at his face. Frowning at his chin, she said, 'Do you need me to pick you up a razor?'

Gareth touched his stubble and said no, he had a razor with him.

'All right,' said Caroline, turning away, patting her pockets to see that she had everything she needed. When the door closed behind her, Gareth headed towards the kitchen; he could hear his daughter's voice and paused outside, listening.

'I wanted to go to the catacombs,' she said.

'I know you did,' said Lionel. 'I will take you there.'

'The sewers!' Rebecca said. 'Why would he take me to the sewers?'

Gareth heard Lionel laughing. He entered the kitchen. The two of them were at the breakfast bar – Rebecca had her back to him, but Lionel saw him and asked, 'How did you sleep?'

Gareth rubbed his face and made a non-committal noise.

Lionel poured him a cup of coffee and gestured towards the breakfast items laid out on the counter. 'Everything is here. You can help yourself,' he said as he left the room. Rebecca reached for the jam, and Gareth watched her spreading her circles of toasted baguette.

He said, 'I've got a riddle for you.' Rebecca had always liked riddles when she was little. 'I never was, am always to be; no one ever saw me, nor ever will. What am I?'

Rebecca pointed to her mouth, which she had just filled, to indicate that she could not talk to him. Lionel came back into the kitchen. He said to Gareth, 'Do you need to borrow my razor?'

'I have a razor,' said Gareth.

'Are you trying to grow a beard?' asked Lionel. 'When you dive, it will interfere with the seal on your mask. Your mask will leak.'

Rebecca stood up, still chewing, and put her plate into the sink.

'You look tired,' said Lionel, observing Gareth.

Through the last of the food in her mouth, Rebecca said, 'We can just stay in, if you're tired.'

'I'm not tired,' said Gareth.

'You *look* tired,' said Rebecca.

'We can watch a film,' said Lionel. A *feelm*. He made a few suggestions to Rebecca, to which she responded enthusiastically.

'We can watch a film this evening, Rebecca,' said Gareth, 'but I wanted to spend today doing something together.'

'We can watch a film *together*,' said Rebecca.

Gareth could not stress in front of Lionel that his plans for the day had not included him. 'We don't have to go to the sewers,' he said. 'We could just go for a walk by the river.'

'Maybe next time,' said Rebecca, who was already going with Lionel into the living room.

With one hand clutching his untouched cup of coffee and the other scratching at his itchy stubble, Gareth said quietly to himself, 'Tomorrow. I'm tomorrow.' He looked at the coffee liqueur that he had brought to give to Caroline, and which Lionel had taken from him; it was out on the counter, not yet opened. Gareth took a slug of his coffee, unscrewed the cap and topped up his cup. He went through to the living room, where the film was already playing. Rebecca was on the two-seater sofa; Lionel was sitting beside her, holding the remote control.

Gareth sat down in the armchair, but he found that he could not follow the film – he was distracted by Lionel, who laughed too often and too loudly. Gareth returned to the kitchen for more coffee, and before the film was halfway through, he had left the flat.

He walked in the direction of the Seine and then took the metro to Pont de l'Alma, the stop for the sewers. He was not far from the Eiffel Tower. A few years before, he had taken Rebecca up the Eiffel Tower, or part of the way up. The structure was never meant to be permanent, he had told her; it was always supposed to be temporary, but it had been standing strong, this wrought iron tower, for well over a century now.

'I know,' she had said, sounding like a teenager even then. 'I live here, remember?'

On the first level of the Eiffel Tower, there was a glass floor, on which they stood, looking down at the ground below, and Gareth, with a little bounce, said, 'I hope it's strong.' On the second level, they joined the snaking queue for the lift that would take them to the very top. After shuffling almost to the front of the queue, Gareth realised that they had the wrong tickets; they would have to pay extra to take the lift to the top. In order to pay, he would have to leave his place in the queue and go and find the right booth, and he could not leave Rebecca there as a place-holder, at her age (*could he?* he thought, eyeing his daughter and the strangers around her). There was not time to start queuing all over again; he had to get her back to Lionel's flat at a reasonable hour. He gave up their place, and as they walked back down the length of the queue, Gareth tried to explain to Rebecca what had happened. 'They should have put up signs near the *start* of the queue,' he said, before seeing that they had in fact put up plenty of signs. On the stairs that took them back down to ground level, Rebecca kept asking, 'But why, why can't we go to the top?' and in the end, Gareth had been reduced to saying, 'Because we can't.' By the time they reached the metro, she had fallen silent. As they travelled through the tunnels, Gareth closed his eyes and could have slept. When he heard Rebecca telling him, 'This is where we get off,' he was sorry to have to open them again; he had no desire to leave the underground, to return to daylight and Lionel's flat.

He had been walking for a while now without paying attention to his route. Looking around, he realised that he had no idea where he was, other than that he was outside a bar. He went inside. He sat down at the bar and drank a beer, and during his second one he told the barman about Lionel. 'You'd think she was *his* daughter. And the way he laughs—' Mostly the barman listened without speaking, but he seemed to understand. There were other customers as well, visible here and there in the dimly lit room; the barman came and went, and Gareth felt himself relaxing. He ought to stop at two, he thought, and get back to the flat, but he found himself ordering a third, which arrived with a shot. 'I wanted to take her to the catacombs,' said Gareth, 'but they're closed.' He downed the shot. It was getting gloomy outside and Gareth wondered if it would rain and then he realised that it was just late; he had lost track of time. But he saw no harm in staying in the tranquillity of the bar for a while longer.

'Yes,' said the barman. 'But you can still go down, if you want to go alone. You are in the right place.' The barman lifted a hatch in the bar and beckoned to Gareth, who got down off his stool, carefully, as if testing the ground's stability. Behind the bar, the barman was lifting up another hatch, in the floor. He led Gareth down through the opening, down a flight of rickety wooden steps, into a cramped cellar. It smelt of stone and dust and alcohol. The barman was over by the far wall, shifting stacked cases of wine, behind which – Gareth could now see – the cellar extended, although it was bare and unlit back there, and seemed to narrow, like the neck of a bottle. The barman gestured for Gareth to go on through the hole he had made. Gareth stepped into this previously hidden part of the cellar, whose narrowing made it more like a passageway really, or a tunnel. He had a years-old memory of being in an extensive wine cellar whose cool, dim corridor of exquisite and collectable bottles went on and on. He tried to recall where it was, that wine cellar, and then realised that he was only remembering a dream in which, as he walked on, the rows of dark bottles to either side of him became rows of gravestones, as old and cold to the touch as the bottles.

The passageway seemed to be sloping downwards, the way the Dartford Tunnel sloped to take him under the

Thames every time he made the trip to Paris, and every time he drove back north. Gareth was still talking to the barman – 'the smell of his cigarette smoke in the bedroom' – when he realised that he was on his own; the barman had other customers upstairs of course. Later, he would thank him for giving him access to what he assumed was the network of underground tunnels that he had heard of – the ancient mines, of which the catacombs were only a small part. These tunnels had started caving in a couple of hundred years ago, and Gareth did not know how far they extended. Nor was he sure quite where within the network the catacombs were, but he felt sure that he was bound, at any moment, to come face to face with a wall of skulls, a wall of bones. He thought of how he would like to go back and say to Rebecca, in front of Lionel, that he had found a secret passageway into the catacombs, except he did not really want to go back there at all.

In darkness now, he inched his hands along the crumbly walls, feeling his way forward through the cold tunnels. He said aloud, 'I will take you there,' and heard the words echo. The roof of the ever-narrowing tunnel scraped against his scalp and he had to stoop. He could not tell whether he was still heading down or starting to go up. Where the tunnel appeared to fork, he took what seemed, from his blind exploration, the easier way, although he soon found that it sloped sharply downwards. When it forked again, he wondered whether he would be able to find his way back if he wanted to. In that airless corridor, there was no promise of light. He could not even see his own hands. He ought to turn back.

Summerside

THE IRVINGS HAD acquired 'Summerside' unseen in an auction, paying a paltry sum for this run-down Victorian property. They found the house unbearable over the winter, but even when the spring came round, it was no better. If anything, it was growing colder. They tried changing the curtains and painting the walls. Mr Irving favoured something bright, a happy shade of yellow. His wife wanted white or magnolia; the closer to white the better, she said. They settled in the middle, with a pale yellow, 'wheat'. But when they looked at it on the walls, they wondered if it was bright enough.

They had an extension built, and in due course they locked the door between it and the old house, living only in the extension and just trying to ignore the other part. As winter approached again, though, they vacated the premises altogether, moving in with Mrs Irving's parents on the far side of the village.

They decided to let the extension. They had, after all, to recoup the money it had cost them to build it.

Mr Irving, showing Anna Harris around the outside

of the property, tried to explain about the old, locked-up part of the house. 'No central heating,' he said.

'It's standing empty?' said Anna.

No, said Mr Irving, it wasn't empty. All the furniture was still in there. It had been left just as it was. Anna thought of the war, of air-raid sirens that meant people had to go quickly to a shelter without stopping for anything, and fire drills at school when you had to get out without even collecting your bag.

She put her face close to the kitchen window, cupped her hands around her eyes and peered through. Mr Irving told her about wanting yellow and his wife wanting white and settling for 'wheat' and then looking at it on the walls and wondering if it was bright enough, if it was bright enough to make the room happy.

'Happy?' said Anna. 'You thought the room was unhappy?'

'You know what I mean. The house as a whole,' said Mr Irving, gesturing towards its dismal facade – Anna thought he had said, 'The house is a hole,' and she nodded, looking at the tatty window frames, the broken stone step – 'is rather impressive, but it has been neglected. Let me show you the new extension.'

He took her to another door that let them into the extension, into the living area. Mr Irving indicated the sofa that folded out into a bed, and the television. He showed her the kitchen, which was really a utility room with a sink, a microwave oven, a portable hob like the one Mitchell took camping, and a kettle. There was no bathroom but there was an outside toilet that was, said Mr Irving, just fine.

'But isn't there a proper bathroom in the old part of the house?' said Anna. 'Isn't there a proper kitchen?'

'There *is*,' said Mr Irving, 'but that's all locked up now.'

'Can they really not be used? Are you saying it's condemned?'

'It's not condemned,' said Mr Irving, 'but you wouldn't want to use them. I'll show you the outside toilet.'

Anna moved in. The lack of space was not a problem because she was not bringing very much with her. A coat cupboard doubled as a wardrobe. The windowsills were her bookshelves. Each morning, she folded away her bed, and ate her breakfast at the little coffee table in the living area. She washed in the utility room. It was like being young again, she thought, just starting out in the world with what little you have.

'I'm on my own now,' she told herself, taking a deep breath. 'I'm making a new start.' She had left behind a life that was not good for her – an unhealthy relationship, an unpleasant job, a polluted town. *You'll never leave Mitchell*, her sister had said. But look at her now; she had done it, she had left him.

Or if you do, you'll go back.

It would soon be a new year and Anna was making plans. She would try again to read *Ulysses*. She would visit art galleries; she would take a beginner's course in Art History so that she could understand the paintings she saw.

Had she been buying rather than renting, she might have taken a lodger, for the company. 'But you wouldn't want to live with a stranger, would you?' said her sister, on the phone from Spain. Anna would have liked to live with her sister, but her sister had emigrated, starting a new life with a man Anna did not like. He reminded her of their father. 'Have you seen Mitchell?' asked her sister. 'I bet you go back to him in the end.'

Lying awake in the fold-out bed, Anna listened to the radio. At one o'clock in the morning, the lady on the radio said, 'Sleep tight,' and Anna switched off her lamp and went to sleep.

Standing at the sink the next morning, washing herself with a flannel, Anna thought: *What I want is a bath.* She wanted to slip into hot water, to feel her muscles unknot, to wash away the world. She went to the door that stood between her and the old house. She put her eye to the keyhole and looked through, seeing the pale yellow of a kitchen wall. She could hear something. Still crouching, she listened to the rhythmic knocking sound. With her mouth close to the door, she said, 'Hello?' She was in a rather uncomfortable position and could not hold it. As she straightened up again, she saw a small boy run past her window. Drawing aside the net curtain, she looked out at the garden. She thought of it as a garden even though it was slabbed. She saw this boy, who was perhaps six years old, circling the house, hitting the walls of the old part with a stick. She moved towards the door but she couldn't go out because she was still naked, holding a flannel in her hand. She picked up the phone and dialled Mr Irving's number. She was going to ask him about the boy but when he answered she said to him, 'I want a bath.'

'I'm afraid,' said Mr Irving, 'I can't let you use the bathroom; I can't let you into the old house.'

Anna finished washing with her flannel at the sink.

◊

She was in the utility room again at lunchtime when she saw that the boy had come back. She had been spreading oatcakes with low-fat cheese (she was trying not to eat bread, not to eat wheat, because it left her bloated, left her feeling bad inside). The boy was standing on the broken doorstep, hitting the old front door with his stick. Anna went outside and said to the boy, as she approached him, 'What are you doing?'

'Waking the ghosts up,' he said, turning to look at her. 'What are *you* doing?'

Anna wondered what he meant, and then she saw that he was looking at how she was walking; he was watching how she stepped carefully over each crack in the paving slabs.

'Oh,' said Anna, smiling. 'Don't you know about the monsters that live under the cracks? If you step on the cracks, they come out and get you.'

Now they were both standing outside the old part of the house, next to the door, which Anna reached out and touched. She put her hand on the handle and turned it, although she could not have said why; she knew that the door was locked and had been locked for months. The door did not open. Anna bent down, opened up the letterbox and looked through. She had a sense of old air getting out, touching her face like warm breath; there was a smell like vegetable soup.

When she stood up again, the boy had run off.

Every wash with her flannel at the sink in the utility room increased Anna's craving for a bath. When she stood at the locked internal door, it was as if she could feel the bathroom's humidity pressing against the wood, as if she could smell bath salts leaking through the keyhole and the cracks. She kept thinking about how it would feel to climb into a full, hot tub. She did not have the key to the door, though, and in the end she had to force it, causing some damage to the frame.

Carrying a towel, shampoo and soap, she stepped through into the old kitchen. She looked around, seeing a fine stove, a family-sized table. *Summerside*, she thought; a lovely name for a family home. She stood and listened to the quiet house. (*Summercide*, she thought, like matricide and patricide and suicide.) She moved further into the room. She saw the wheat-coloured walls and felt nauseous, bad inside. That pale shade of yellow was not enough. The stale air filled her nostrils, her mouth, her throat and lungs.

She walked towards the stairs.

If anyone knocked on the door of the extension in the weeks that followed, they went away again without an answer, until rent day came around again and Mr Irving arrived looking for Anna. Letting himself into the living area, he found the internal door broken open. Not wanting to step into the old house on his own, he fetched his brothers.

He is going to let the extension again – he can't afford not to – but he will impress upon his new tenant that the old house is out of bounds. He has not mentioned his previous tenant's breaking and entering, her being found drowned in the bath. He has mended the door frame.

As he hands Katie McKinsey the key, receiving in return a cheque – her deposit and a month's rent in advance – he notices that the boy, that damned boy, is hanging around again. He was a nuisance when Mr Irving and his wife lived here. They had to keep chasing him off the property. Mr Irving would shoo him away but Katie McKinsey seems delighted by him. Mr Irving knows that she is alone and has no children.

Katie keeps asking about using the kitchen. 'I like to cook,' she says, standing outside the old house now, turning towards the kitchen window. 'I like to bake cakes.'

'You can make cakes in the microwave in the utility room,' says Mr Irving.

Katie is at the window, peering into the kitchen with her hands cupped around her eyes. 'I bet you like cakes,' she says, turning to look at the boy, who is stamping about on the paving slabs, or, rather, on the cracks between them. 'Watch out,' she tells him, 'you don't want to wake up the bears!'

'There aren't any bears,' says the boy. 'And I don't think it's monsters either, but there's something down there.'

'Is that right?' says Katie, standing outside her new home with the key in her hand, and she laughs, but no one else does, and after a while she stops.

Fidelity

GINA DOUBTS SHE'LL be able to sleep now. There is light in the sky and the birds have started up. Birds unnerve her, even garden birds – perhaps especially garden birds, because they're so close. They perch in the little tree outside and shit on the patio. They are on the roof and in the eaves, and their noise bursts in through the open window.

She came to bed late, after drinking too much at the wake. When the last people had said their goodbyes and *You know where we are*, Gina had been left with the plates of half-eaten food to refrigerate or throw away, and she had done neither, just abandoned it where it was and came to bed and turned on the radio to have the graveyard shift for company.

At some point, she must have dropped off, because she remembers the shock, coming out of some dream, hearing Spiritualized on the radio, hearing, of all things, 'I Think I'm in Love', which was her and Martin's song. It was as if the DJ, working through the small hours with his blood full of caffeine, had tapped into something, as if the universe itself were reaching out to Gina, like a mother to her hurt or worried child, saying *I'm here.*

Gina has been awake since then. She has turned the radio off.

Martin played that song for her the first time she went round to his flat. 'Listen to this,' he said, and he meant it: he wanted her to sit in silence from the start to the end of the eight-minute track. She kept talking, and he kept saying, 'Ssh, listen.' He wanted her to love it too, and when the track ended she said yeah, she liked it. She wasn't sure if it was a love song, but it became their song anyway. She lies alone in their bed, remembering wanting him. They worked together at a magazine. His flat was closer to the office, so it made sense for her to move in with him. He played that track a lot, also 'Stay with Me' and 'Broken Heart'.

The magazine job was good while it lasted, really great in fact, but the company collapsed in the recession. Now Gina works for the county council.

On the Monday, she returns to work. Every call she takes seems to be a problem or a complaint; every caller seems angry. By home time, she's feeling bludgeoned. She dumps her bag on the kitchen counter and opens the fridge, takes out a bottle of white. Martin used to nag her about this, about her drinking the moment she came home, or about her drinking with colleagues after work instead of coming home. And then of course she would call him boring, and when he had finished sulking he would say, 'Who was there?' and she'd avoid mentioning the men.

She finishes the wine and takes a bath – a warm bath with bubbles, in candlelight – and when she gets out she's so sleepy she goes straight to bed, early like a sick or naughty child. She is woken in the dark by Alison Moyet singing 'Is This Love?', though Gina has no memory of switching the radio on.

'Who was there?' he had asked.

'The girls,' said Gina. 'You know.'

'The girls,' said Martin. 'Rebecca?'

'Yes,' said Gina, turning away to undress. 'Anna's thinking of—'

'Rebecca called here,' said Martin.

'Hmm?' said Gina, pulling on her nightdress.

'Rebecca called here.'

'When?' said Gina.

'While you were out,' said Martin. 'She called to see if you were all right. She said it's not like you to go straight home from work. She thought there might be something wrong, like maybe you were ill.'

Gina picked up her hairbrush, looking into the mirror to brush out her hair. When she turned around to face him, he'd already gone to bed.

She bags up his clothes for charity. She takes sackful after sackful down to the British Heart Foundation. And still she finds things: his favourite shirt somehow overlooked in his side of the wardrobe; his walking boots next to hers in the hallway, and, when she has got rid of those, his flip flops. She drops these things off at the clothing bin near the county council office. After work, she goes for a drink with Liam and comes out slightly over the limit. Getting into her car to drive home, she glances, for some reason, at the back seat, and finds Martin's tie, which must have come out of the bag. He only ever had one tie, with Mickey Mouse on it. He'd worn it to at least one job interview and to weddings and funerals; it had become something of a joke, how inappropriate it was. She ought, really, to have had him cremated in it. She shuts it into the glove compartment and goes home to bed, falling asleep listening to a talk radio station. She nearly makes it through to morning, and perhaps it is the dawn chorus that wakes her, or perhaps it is 'Caught Out There', which is playing on the radio.

Their anniversary weekend away had been sprung on her at the last minute. It was very thoughtful of him – two nights in a country house in the Cotswolds – but she did not like surprises, and he knew that. She looked it up online: it had a spa, 'so you can get treatments,' he said. She said it sounded really nice and asked what time they'd need to leave, and he said, 'After work.'

'But what time?'

'I mean, right after work,' he said. 'You finish at five, right? So you can be home by half past? We'll go then.'

They didn't work together any more: Gina used the car for her commute, and Martin worked from home. They would pack the night before, he said, and when Gina got home at half past five they would put their suitcases into the car and drive to the Cotswolds.

'I have a meeting on Friday,' said Gina.

'After five o'clock?' said Martin.

'It starts at five,' said Gina. 'It shouldn't go on too long.'

'Well, get home as soon as you can,' said Martin. 'It's a two-hour drive and we want to be there in time for dinner.'

She did her best, and was home before seven, and if Martin smelt the pub on her he did not mention it, and if he had mentioned it she would just have said that's where the meeting was, and that would not even be a lie. They were almost at the country house – late for dinner, the light gone – when Martin reached into the back, feeling around for his cardigan, finding a tie. 'Whose tie is this?' he asked, bringing it into the front.

'Oh,' said Gina, glancing at it and then looking back at the road. 'It must be yours.'

Martin switched on the interior light, making it painfully obvious there was no Mickey Mouse on the tie.

At work, she is given some leeway. They are as understanding as they can be when Gina is unfocused, distracted, short-tempered, and when she turns up late, and makes mistakes, and seems to be losing the plot.

At home, she's been leaving the radio off, but still it wakes her in the small hours, the mean hours, the dead of night, playing 'Shame on You'. She doesn't know who's singing. She looks it up and finds at least three recent tracks with this name, also 'Shame on U' which is much older and sung in French except for the eponymous chorus. There are so many different versions, so many different ways of saying it. She unplugs the radio.

When, at dawn, the chorus of 'I Hate Everything About You' kicks in like an alarm, she takes out the batteries.

She thinks she might be dreaming this music, because a talk radio station does not play songs, and a radio cannot just turn itself on, but nonetheless she puts the radio, unplugged and emptied of batteries, in the hallway, ready for charity.

The problem, she tells herself, is how lonely it is to wake in their bed in the dark with so much of the night still to come. The mind plays tricks then. She remembers, in childhood, making a den in the hollow of an old tree. She had put down some carpet, an offcut, and crouched on this uneven rug to eat her raisins, pretending that this was her dinner, that this cold hollow was her home. A boy she was playing with wanted a door, and barricaded the opening with plywood, shutting out the light, shutting the two of them in. It was so dark, so unbearably dark, and Gina, feeling small fingers in her hair, said, 'Open the door.' 'No,' said the boy, who was nowhere near her. Hours later, back at home, in her bed, with a night light on, she could not close her eyes without expecting to feel – in her hair, on her scalp, on some exposed part of her – the creep of bony fingers.

She has explained so many times – to his parents, to his sister, to their friends – that she had no idea, when she left for the team-building weekend, that Martin was so ill. Yes, he had been sleeping a lot, and he had been complaining of feeling the cold, but she had told him to go to the doctor if it got too much worse, or, seeing as she had the car, she could take him there herself when she got back, and she promised to phone.

But he couldn't get out of bed, said his mother. *He could*, said Gina. He *did* get out of bed, when he needed the toilet or a hot drink or some soup, or when he wanted the window shut. They had fought over that: him wanting the window closed – 'I'm so cold,' he said, 'I'm really cold' – and her wanting it open because she did not want his germs. They were arguing right before she left, plus it was a really long drive to Scotland, where the activity weekend was, which is why she didn't phone that first day. And then, the next day, it was really full-on and there honestly wasn't a moment to think about anything that wasn't hiking or rafting; they just didn't stop until the evening, when they had a barbeque.

She texted him from the barbeque. She didn't phone – she has explained this – because it might wake him up and he needed to sleep, he was sleeping nearly round the clock, and he needed that, she thought, to recover. Even then, when he texted back, the first thing he asked was, 'Who else is there?' She did not even reply.

She texted again the following evening, in response to a message he'd left in the night. *No*, she said, *I'll be home tomorrow, not sure what time.* And then Liam was there with a drink and a smile, saying, 'Domestic discord?' and she said, ''fraid so,' and smiled back and turned off her phone.

The one time she brings Liam home, it feels as if she is sneaking a boyfriend into the family home, as if there might be someone there she does not want to disturb.

They're a bit drunk. Bringing Liam into the hallway, Gina is shushing him, and Liam thinks this is funny. And Gina, tripping over the radio, supposes it is.

She goes giggling into the en suite bathroom and when she comes out Liam's in the bed, on Martin's side, waiting for her. She's glad he's there. She wants the company. She thinks how nice it will be to have him there with her in the early hours.

During the night she opens her eyes. She can hear music, though it *cannot* be coming from the empty radio abandoned in the hallway. She senses Liam's wakefulness too; he reaches for her, and she feels his fingers on her skin and then in her hair.

'It's really cold,' she says to him. 'Did you open the window?'

'No,' says Liam, from the far side of the room, his dark shape in the bathroom doorway.

The fingers are still in her hair, winding it tight.

The Voice of the People

ON THE DAY of the protest, Glenda decided to drive out to the retail park to buy weedkiller. She was just setting out, getting into third gear, when a pigeon dawdling in the road caused her to brake hard. The pigeon seemed oblivious, even when Glenda's two-tonne car was virtually on top of it. Perhaps the car actually was on top of it, because having stopped dead, Glenda could not see the pigeon anywhere. She was just about to get out to look beneath her wheels when she saw the pigeon wandering to the side of the road. She watched its strangely sluggish progress, and then drove on, towards the edge of the village.

The garden was really Dougie's responsibility, but work was taking it out of him these days. On his day off, he just lay on the sofa, with the cat asleep on top of him, or sometimes the cat fell asleep on the carpet or in the lengthening grass, wherever it happened to be. Dougie himself did not really sleep, but just lay there, with no energy for Glenda, or for his projects: at the far end of the overgrown garden, a half-dug pond had been abandoned, and the second-hand furniture that he had bought to spruce up was gathering dust in the spare room. The last piece he had done was the little table on which their telephone stood: he had spent weeks sanding and then staining and varnishing it, although Glenda hated it, the darkness of its wood, and its rickety, skeletal legs.

She had just got onto a faster stretch of road leading out of the village when another pigeon staggered out in front of her car, not even flinching away from the vehicle as she skimmed past. She wondered what was wrong with these pigeons; they were like zombies.

It was not just Dougie; it seemed to be everyone who worked at that factory. They had all lost their pep. No one in the village liked the factory, although the men needed the jobs; it employed hundreds of them. It was an ugly, stony-faced building, ruining what had been a nice stretch of riverside, at a spot where the locals used to swim – some still did, but not many. The women had been worrying about the factory's emissions, about what exactly was going into the air. Sometimes the smoke that went into the clouds looked yellow. And was anything going into the river, anything that should not be? Dougie used to fish there, but he did not do that any more. And there was that terrible smell, which had to be coming from the factory.

At the bend, where the road turned away from the river, there was a pigeon, flattened against the tarmac. Its grey wings were splayed around its crushed body. Its underbelly was turned up to face the sky, to face the wheels of the oncoming traffic. These pigeons reminded Glenda of the summer outbreak of flying ants, which did not fly off at the flap of a hand as houseflies did; or they reminded her of the houseflies themselves, the listlessness that came over them at the end of the summer, leaving them too slow to avoid the swatter. But she had never before noticed the phenomenon in birds or other creatures.

Glenda had written the council a letter, which the other women had signed. The letter asked questions about those emissions; it suggested that the factory might be affecting the health of the workers; it requested a thorough investigation and the suspension of operations pending the results. The men had not signed the letter. The letter had been forwarded to a secretary who would liaise with the relevant committee; it was then, after somebody's holiday, to be discussed at a forthcoming meeting. Not having heard anything for a while, Glenda had left messages on a council answerphone. In the meantime, the women were going to go on a protest march. 'We never used to take things lying down,' Glenda had said to the women. 'When we were students, we used to march.' They used to go down to London, on coaches; they had marched through the capital in their thousands, to force things to change. 'We *should*,' the women had said in response. 'We *should* do that.' Since then, they had been meeting every Wednesday morning at Fiona's house. Fiona had provided refreshments while they made placards, nailing boards to wooden sticks and painting slogans on them – WE WANT ANSWERS! – slogans that they would shout as they marched. They had photocopied flyers to put through people's letterboxes. They had notified the local paper.

Glenda glanced at the dashboard clock. It was almost noon; they were due to meet to start the protest at one o'clock. They would march down Union Street to the river, right down to the factory. They would stand outside that grim building and stamp their feet and shout, make some noise. Someone would have to respond; something would have to be done.

She pulled into the car park of the DIY store, disturbing a couple of birds, which flapped up into the air and flew away. She parked near the entrance and went inside the store. As she entered the gardening section, she recognised a neighbour who was standing looking at the lawnmowers. Glenda said hello. She could not think of her neighbour's name. The woman continued to stare at a lawnmower, and Glenda thought that she had not heard her, but then the woman said, 'I've been here for hours. I just can't decide.'

'Are you coming on the protest?' asked Glenda.

'I just can't decide,' said the woman.

Glenda turned away and picked up a spray-gun bottle of ready-to-use weedkiller. She took it over to the till, where the cashier was sharing a joke with a man who had bought paint in a shade called 'Nursery'. The colour looked putrid to Glenda. The man turned away and the cashier looked at Glenda and said, 'Are you all right?'

'I'm fine,' said Glenda, lifting her free hand and touching her face. 'It's just a rash.' She handed over the weedkiller and the cashier scanned it. Glenda looked at the silver and copper in her purse. She could not be bothered to count out the coins. She handed over a note and waited for her change, and then stood struggling with the zip of her purse. She took her weedkiller and moved towards the exit, aware of the cashier watching her as she walked away.

She strapped the weedkiller into the passenger seat, as if it were a child. She did not want it sliding around, busting open, weedkiller going everywhere. She drove home slowly, carefully.

41

It was after one o'clock when she returned to the outskirts of the village, where she found Fiona sitting on the kerb, with a placard on the pavement beside her. Glenda came to a stop and wound down her window. She said to Fiona, 'Have they gone already?'

Fiona raised her eyes. 'Who?'

'The other women,' said Glenda. 'Have they started the march?'

'No one else has turned up,' said Fiona.

'Oh,' said Glenda. 'Well, I have to take the car home, then I'm going to walk back down here and join you. Even if it's just the two of us, we can still march down to the factory. We can still make some noise.' She drove home, passing a car that was so badly parked it looked as if it had just been abandoned mid-manoeuvre, and stopping to move a child's bike that had been left lying across the road. She backed her car into a kerbside space and took the weedkiller inside. She put on some sunscreen and checked her appearance in the mirror. She was wearing the olive-green eyeliner that Dougie had once said brought alive her copper-coloured eyes, but now she wondered if it was just making her look a bit ill. She put down some food for the cat. By the time she got back down to the corner with her placard, Fiona was no longer there. Glenda thought about going to the factory anyway, on her own, but she did not really think she had the energy.

When Glenda got home again, she filled a glass with water from the tap, and drank it standing at the sink. It was past lunchtime, but she was not hungry, and there was still food in the cat's bowl from before. She went through to the lounge and sat down in an armchair, next to the second-hand table with the phone on it. She had disliked that table, she thought, but now she could not really see what was wrong with it; she did not have any strong feelings about it either way. Next to the phone were her phone numbers. There was the number for the council – she would have to call them again at some point, about that letter she had sent to them. And there was Fiona's number – she ought to call her; she ought to call everyone. The protest would have to be rescheduled. The numbers seemed to blur; she must be tired. She switched on the TV and watched the afternoon programmes. She was still sitting there when Dougie came in from the factory. He lay down on the sofa.

'Have you seen the cat?' asked Glenda.

'Uh-uh,' said Dougie.

In between TV programmes, Glenda said, 'I'm going to go up to bed,' but she did not actually move for a while.

Eventually, she got to the bathroom and picked up her toothbrush. She looked at herself in the mirror. It felt like being stared at by a stranger. Her eyes were the colour of dull pennies. She left the bathroom and got into bed. She looked at her book but she felt that she just wanted to sleep. She realised that she had somehow not cleaned her teeth after all. She thought about her unbrushed teeth rotting in the night, but she did not get up again; she just left them.

A week and a half later, Glenda found the cat beneath the back wheel of her car, against the kerb. It must not have moved out of the way when Glenda was parking. She had not been anywhere since the previous weekend, when she went to fetch that weedkiller.

She stood at the kerb, trying to remember what she

had come outside for. There was no point driving over to Fiona's house: the group had dissolved.

Glenda's placard was still propped against the front wall. She picked it up, looking at the faded lettering: WE WANT ANSWERS! Had she written that? It did not sound like her, like something she would say. Perhaps she had got somebody else's placard by mistake. She stood on the pavement, near the kerb. She could see the factory chimney in the distance, down by the river, belching its mustard smoke into the sky. Dougie would be taking his lunch break soon. She could walk down there and try to see him, see if he was feeling any better. If she found, on the way, that she did not want to keep carrying the placard, which may or may not have been hers, she could just leave it somewhere.

She stepped into the road, with the sign hanging down, the message (WE WANT ANSWERS!) dangling in the gutter. She moved out into the road, slowly, as if she were stepping through the mud at the edge of the river, mud in which Dougie had seen fish lying belly up.

She did have a sense of the size and weight of the vehicle that was coming towards her. She was not oblivious to the juggernaut that was bearing down on her. But it felt more peripheral, more distant, than it was. She was moving forward, looking towards the far side of the road, but with no great sense of urgency.

Seabound

MAY HAD SPENT her entire life in that clifftop house. She did not remember a time when she had not known Dylan, who lived next door when they were young. Dylan was older though. May tagged along when he went down to the beach, which was where he liked to be, peering into the rock pools or wading into the waves, looking for ships.

While May was still at the local secondary school, Dylan was already working, and talking about getting away from this dead-end place. He wanted – he had always wanted – to go to sea.

'I don't want you to go,' said May.

'But one of these days,' he said, 'I will go.'

May did her best to keep him with her. When she told him she loved him, he said he loved her too. When she told him she would always love him, he said, 'Come here,' and stroked her hair. When she told him she was having his baby, he said, 'You're welcome to have it, but you'll be on your own.' He was joining the navy; he had already been accepted.

May tried to persuade him not to leave, but it was like

throwing coins into a wishing well: she could throw in all the coins she liked and tell him all her wishes but it would not make them come true. 'I love you,' she insisted. 'You said you loved me.'

'I *do* love you,' he said, but at the same time, he was putting on his boots. May believed he did love her in a way, but she was not the sea, which was where he really wanted to be, which was where he felt he belonged.

While Dylan was beginning his life at sea, May was giving birth to Daisy. She continued to live with her parents, raising Daisy in that clifftop house and waiting for Dylan to come home. And he did return, from time to time, for a few weeks every year, seeing his parents, seeing May, and Daisy, who was shy of him.

Daisy never called him Dad; she called him Dylan, when she called him anything at all. She was stiffly polite towards him, as if he were an especially important or unwelcome guest. Occasionally, Daisy lowered her guard and befriended him, and then he left again. He never wrote letters, never phoned. As a young adult, Daisy sometimes refused to see him, and when she moved away – when her career took her inland – she ceased to see him at all.

After giving his best years to the sea, Dylan retired. His parents were no longer living, and even their house was long gone, but May was just where he had left her, and she took him in. He had no more possessions than he could carry on his back. He often fell asleep in an armchair, with his clothes and shoes still on, as if he were ready to leave at any moment. He'd barely returned to dry land when his heart gave out.

After the funeral, Daisy asked her mum to move inland, to live with her.

'I've spent my whole life here,' said May. 'All my memories are here. All my things are here.' She felt at home, in that house on the cliff edge against which the sea beat.

Daisy phoned every few days to see how she was, and May said she was fine.

Except sometimes she was troubled in the night. All alone in the big bed that had once belonged to her parents, May dreamt she stood in the shallows at the edge of the sea, which sucked the sand from beneath her feet. She went deeper. Vast and cold, the sea climbed her bare legs. It was rough, but she stood her ground. Sometimes, when she woke from these dreams, the sea was so loud it could have been right there in her room.

Daisy phoned. She said she was redecorating the guest bedroom, and sent a picture of the wallpaper she was going to put up. May eyed her own wallpaper, which had probably been there as long as she had, along with the curtains, faded by sunlight, and the carpets, worn thin. Her window frames could do with repainting, or replacing; double glazing might help. But redecorating would mean having to move everything. The house was full of stuff, unused things, unread books. She was a hoarder.

The dreams got worse. She dreamt there was a man made of water, who came to her house in the night. She heard his wet feet in the hallway, and on the stairs as he climbed to her room. He came to her bedside. Really, he was just the *shape* of a man, an *idea* of a man, a disruption in the darkness, but she knew he was there. Sometimes she woke from these strange dreams to find her nightie and her bedding damp and smelling of salt.

She put her nightie and her bedding into the washing machine, and opened a window to get some air into the room. She looked out at the garden, which had once been extensive, but over the years so much had been lost. The sea was hurling itself at the cliff face. Its spray, carried on the wind, flung itself against the walls of her house. She closed the window again.

Daisy phoned. She told her mum she worried about her, and May said she was fine. But the erosion was getting worse, said Daisy, who saw how the sea was clawing its way towards the foundations of that clifftop house. She did not want her mother to be one of those people refusing to budge even as the house she was living in was falling into the sea.

There was damp in the walls. It was coming through the bedroom wallpaper, on which mould, black mould, was spreading so stubbornly she could not keep it at bay. The walls would have to be stripped and treated.

'It's bad for your health,' said Daisy.

'I know,' said May.

When, at night, the seaman came, moving through darkness or moonlight to her bedside, she knew he was looking for something. He did not seem to see her. She asked him, 'Is it me you want?' and then, in the silence, 'What do you want?' He did not seem to hear her. What troubled her – as he came closer, looking, wanting, not seeing her, not hearing her – was that she knew perfectly well what he had wanted all along.

◊

May opened the little dark-wood cupboard next to her bed and removed the urn of ashes. He had wanted his remains to be scattered at sea. Even Daisy knew that, and had asked her mother from time to time if she had done it yet, and May had had to say no, not yet, until eventually she had said yes, she had done it, it was done, and hoped that would be the end of it.

May carried the urn downstairs. She put it on the kitchen table and kept it there while she made her breakfast. She ate lightly. She had never seen much point in cooking for one. She made a pot of tea, and drank the first cup at the table and the second cup at the window. She could see that the wind had dropped. When she put down her empty cup, she said to the urn of ashes, 'All right then.'

She put on her coat and her walking boots and left the house clutching the urn. She walked from the clifftop down to the promenade. People were out and about, alone and in couples and families. It was still cold though. She was almost alone on the beach.

She passed the rock pools, which filled up when the sea came in. It was coming in now. When she reached the shore, she stopped. She took the lid from the urn and, bending down to be closer to the water, poured the ashes into the shallows. She kept her walking boots out of the way. It was oddly like emptying the ash pan after a fire, or even – she did it with such care – pouring flour into the bowl of her kitchen scales to make a cake with Daisy. The sea washed in and out, carrying the ashes away.

When the urn was empty, May replaced the lid. She

stood for a moment and watched the horizon, looking for ships. The clouds drifted by.

She was, she realised, as she turned away and left the beach, quite hungry now.

From the promenade, she could only just see the clifftop house in which she had spent her life so far. Just in front of her was the little cafe to which she used to bring her daughter.

The bell above the door rings as she enters. Inside, it is warm. May chooses a table next to the window and puts the urn by her feet. When someone comes to ask her what she wants, May asks for coffee. It feels like a long time since she slept well. She thinks of her mouldering bedroom, that house full of stuff she doesn't need. While she waits for her coffee to come, she watches the birds: the gulls and the sparrows. She prefers the sparrows. She thinks of the garden birds Daisy has on the wallpaper she's putting up in her guest bedroom. It sounds nice.

First, she will have her cup of coffee, and a look at the menu. Then she will call Daisy, whose number is stored in her mobile phone. She will ask about the guest bedroom. Then she will begin the journey back, knowing, now, that he will not be returning.

The Harvestman

ELIOT WAKES TO find that his arm has gone numb. It is flung back on his pillow, bent beneath his head. He has to move it with his other hand to get the blood back into it. Its dead weight is unsettling. It is as if he has discovered a ten-pound leg of lamb lying on his pillow. Sitting up, holding on to the arm, he waits for it to fizz back to life.

There are no curtains at the window, nothing to buffer the daylight in those first few minutes of being awake. The flat was supposed to be furnished and he has been promised some curtains, but, in the meantime, it doesn't bother him much. His flat is at the top of a three-storey block, so it's not like anyone walking by can peer in. The road that the flats back onto is quiet anyway. The lack of curtains only troubles him if he wakes in the night and sees the cold window with all that darkness outside, that big black rectangle in the middle of the long wall.

Eliot goes over to the window and opens it, leaning on the windowsill and lighting up a cigarette, blowing the smoke outside. The block is an eyesore but those at the front have a view of the sea. Eliot's flat is at the back. The slabbed pavement down below reminds him of a dream he had when he was small, in which he jumped from his bedroom window to the patio slabs underneath and sank, very comfortably, into the ground, as if he were Mr Soft, as if nothing could hurt him. 'It wouldn't be like that though,' his mum had said when he told her about his dream. 'You'd be lucky just to break your legs.'

He gets dressed, pulling on skinny jeans patched at the knees and a sweater with suede patches on the elbows. He heads down to the amusements, half walking, half jogging. 'Always in a hurry,' his mum says of him. Eliot is lanky, all legs. He is like the harvestmen that so unnerve him. Spiders give him the creeps but harvestmen are worse. If a predator gets hold of a harvestman's leg, the harvestman can just detach it and make his escape, leaving the lost leg twitching in the predator's jaw. When Eliot was small, he was easily upset by animals with spindly legs and backwards knees. He remembers seeing an emu at the zoo. Something about the way it ran, the way its legs bent the wrong way, made him cry.

The cold, fresh air in his lungs makes him want another cigarette, so he smokes while he walks, while the tide pulls out.

He spends a couple of hours at the amusements, winning some, losing some. They're advertising for someone to work in the change booth. Every time the manager sees Eliot, he says to him, from the confines of the booth, 'This could be you.' The booth is perhaps three feet wide by three feet deep, and more than six feet tall with perspex windows on three sides. Sitting in there would make him feel like the guy in one of those animatronic fortune-telling machines, like Zoltar, but at least not like Economy Zoltar whose booth is only two feet square and who has no head or arm movement. He would feel like a spider caught under a glass.

At lunchtime, Eliot leaves the amusements with some change in his pockets. He stops to smoke a cigarette on the esplanade. The seaside, with all its trappings, is new and exciting to him. He's spent his life so far on a farm in the north. He had been desperate to get away from home. Even when he was little, he had run away from home, just for the fun of it. That had got him a skin-stinging slap on his bare legs, and his mum had said, 'You've got worse than that coming your way if you ever do it again.' She said he was just like his granddad who had lied about his age so that he could go and fight in the war. 'He was only a boy,' she said, 'but he just couldn't wait to go. You remind me of him.' His granddad went to Ypres, and spent the rest of his long life confined to a wheelchair.

Eliot came south on his motorbike, racing along with the open road ahead of him, reminding himself of his mum going down to Gretna Green with her future a great unknown. Her family had said, at the time, that she was making a mistake, choosing *him* for a boyfriend, a husband, but that just made her want him more. They'd been right though; she had made a bad choice.

His grandmother always believed that travelling south was easier than travelling north because south was 'downhill' on the map, as if anyone trying to go north without concentrating risked rolling all the way back down; as if, in fact, gravity could make anyone tumble down at any moment.

He keeps his motorbike outside the block of flats. He ought to get some proper motorbike leathers, and boots with toe protection and ankle, heel and shin armour. His mum has warned him that he goes too fast, that he'll end up hitting the tarmac at so many miles per hour and then he'll have pins in his legs, 'if you're lucky', she said.

Eliot, leaning on the railings above the beach, watches someone surfing, falling into the rough, grey sea, and he's glad it's not him out there.

He goes into The Hook, where Abbey is serving behind the bar. He wants to say something nice to her, like he likes her top or what she's done with her hair, but when he says that sort of thing to her she just laughs. He asks for a pint and a roll and Abbey knows exactly what he wants – which pint, which roll.

When he reached the seaside – when he came to a stop at the bottom of the country and could go no further – The Hook was the first place he came to. It was how he found his flat, and where he first saw Abbey. When she told him her name, he said, 'As in an abbey?'

'Yes,' she said. 'As in monks.'

Eliot can't think of monks without thinking of sex. Probably he has read too many gothic novels.

Abbey has told him that she likes his accent, which makes him self-conscious when he speaks. He tries not to stare while she pulls the pint, fetches the roll, but he finds it hard not to look at her. When she catches his eye, she smiles. He gets the right money ready to put into her hand. Will Young's 'Leave Right Now' comes on. It's Abbey's favourite song and she plays it all the time, or she does when Eliot's there.

Her boyfriend, Big Pete, has told Eliot to stay away from Abbey, but Big Pete is never around during the day – he works elsewhere – so Eliot sometimes comes into the pub for his lunch. He knows it's not a good idea but he does it anyway.

Big Pete always wears a dark suit – like he is permanently ready for a funeral – with a sheepskin coat on top if it is cold. He is something like a debt collector or a bailiff. Eliot imagines him kicking down doors with those big boots of his, although probably he uses tools; he has tools in his van, maybe specialist tools that Eliot doesn't even know the name of and wouldn't know what they were for if he ever saw them.

'Don't look at Abbey like that,' Big Pete said one night, pushing Eliot up against the side of his van. 'Don't look at Abbey at all,' he added, but that was like saying, 'Don't think about spiders; don't think of harvestmen losing their legs.' Abbey was right there, standing in the doorway of The Hook, and when Big Pete told Eliot not to look at her, Eliot looked at her. Big Pete pressed Eliot harder into the side of his van, though not much harder, not wanting to damage the van. Big Pete's tools make Eliot think of kneecaps. 'Last chance,' said Big Pete, before letting him go.

Big Pete also owns the flats. He owes Eliot some curtains and Eliot owes Big Pete some rent.

Eliot bites into his roll and Abbey says to him, 'You going to the fireworks tonight?' Eliot, with his mouth full, has not answered before Abbey adds, 'I don't think Pete will be there.'

Eliot looks at her.

He strides along the esplanade, where the signs say 'NO CYCLING', 'DON'T WALK ON THE FLOWERBEDS', 'DON'T FEED THE GULLS', 'NO DOGS ON THE ESPLANADE OR THE BEACH'. It is already getting dark. The cold wind is giving him an earache. He struggles to light his cigarette and then smokes it quickly.

He wonders if he'll get home for Christmas. On Boxing Day, the hunt rides through their village and over the surrounding fields, despite the fox-hunting ban. His dad used to go with them, before he fell from his galloping horse and lost the use of his legs, as if there were some hereditary disease affecting the male line, something that would get you whether you stayed close to home or whether you tried to get away.

Eliot nips into the off-licence and then gets some chips from the chippy, eating them on the esplanade. The bonfire's been lit. He wanders down to the beach, passing the 'NO DISABLED ACCESS' sign. Abbey has come out of the pub and is standing near the blazing fire, her face lit by its glow. The old fishing boats are being burnt, like a sacrificial offering on a funeral pyre to appease the vengeful gods. Abbey touches her cheeks as if she is too hot, too close, but she stays where she is. Others are warming their outstretched hands. They remind him of the little girl in the advert for the fireworks code, holding out her burnt and bandaged fingers, and his mum saying, 'That's why we have rules.'

He makes his way towards Abbey. When she sees him, she smiles, and then she turns and smiles at the fire. Eliot takes his quarter bottle of whisky out of his pocket and they pass it between them. The first of the rockets shoots up like a flare at the edge of the sea. On the bonfire, the boats are beginning to catch.

Eliot is putting the empty bottle away when he sees Big Pete marching down the beach in the direction of the bonfire. Hoping that he hasn't been seen, Eliot says to Abbey, 'I'm going to go,' and Abbey, who has spotted him too, nods.

Eliot gets back up onto the esplanade and returns to

the flats. Wider than it is tall, the block of flats looks like a hospital. Some of the residents sit at their windows all day long, watching the waves roll in and out, if they live at the front.

In his room, Eliot opens the window, leans on the sill and lights a cigarette. Despite the season and the weather, he doesn't feel cold; he feels warmed by the whisky; he feels softened.

I don't think Pete will be there, she'd said, and Eliot had looked at her. When Abbey started locking up at three o'clock, Eliot was still sitting at the bar with the end of his second pint. 'You've never seen the flat, have you?' she said. It wasn't exactly an invitation, but he took it as one. He went with her through the door marked 'NO PUBLIC ACCESS', up the stairs and into the flat that she shared with Big Pete. In the kitchen, an apron hanging from a hook said 'Don't Mess With The Chef!' When Eliot turned around, he found himself looking at a tea towel that said the same thing. On the kitchen counter, there was a black-and-white television whose screen showed the empty bar downstairs. Abbey made some instant coffee and they took their mugs into the bedroom so that Eliot could see the view of the beach from there. There was a frilly nightie on her pillow, and on the floor there was an extra-large T-shirt that said 'IT'S HAMMER TIME'.

Abbey lifted her mug to her mouth, spotted the old boats being placed on top of the bonfire and moved to point them out, dribbling coffee down the front of her white top. 'Fuck me,' she said, under her breath, and put her mug down on the windowsill. As she walked over to the wardrobe, she said, 'Don't look.'

Eliot gazed out of the window and listened to Abbey undressing on the far side of the room while he watched the people down on the beach building the bonfire up. 'Can I smoke in here?' he asked.

'No, you can't,' said Abbey, 'or Pete will know you've been in here.' Eliot nodded, drank the last of his coffee and put his mug down next to Abbey's.

Eliot is not allowed to smoke in his own flat either, but he does anyway, the tip of his cigarette glowing orange like a dashboard warning light while he leans over the sill of the open window. He blows out smoke rings and watches as they drift up into the night sky, dispersing. They look like cartoon wailing or surprise: o O O. The ash falling to the ground makes him think of that thing about a feather and a brick descending at exactly the same speed, or a ton of feathers and a ton of bricks. That's in a vacuum though, or on the moon or something.

Hearing a knock at the door to his flat, he turns and is about to cross the room to open up when there's a second, harder knock and Big Pete's voice booms through the door: 'I've got something for you.' Eliot pictures Big Pete standing in the hallway, with tools in his hands or in the big pockets of his sheepskin coat. 'Open up, mate,' says Big Pete. 'Mate' is one of those words that doesn't always mean what it seems to. It might mean you're about to get a smack in the face; it depends on how it's said, like 'love': 'Look, *love*.' 'Look, *mate*.' Into Eliot's head comes an image of the black-and-white closed-circuit television that sits on the kitchen counter in the flat above The Hook, and the video camera that is trained behind the bar and perhaps also – he tries to remember – has a view of the door that says 'NO PUBLIC ACCESS', a surveillance system whose footage Big Pete can watch back any time he likes. Eliot imagines himself and Abbey on the screen, in grainy monochrome, like the CCTV images that you see on the news, crucial or final moments when someone's been attacked or gone missing; Eliot and Abbey going through the door to the private flat above, and – he imagines Big Pete with his thumb on the fast-forward button, his expression hardening – Abbey coming back into the bar a while later, wearing a different top. Eliot thinks about the two used coffee mugs on the windowsill in the bedroom, and the T-shirt that says 'IT'S HAMMER TIME'. *Oh shit*, he thinks.

No one would hear him yelling. Everyone's down on the beach, at the front, looking the other way. He can hear the fireworks, which have reached their climax, their loud cracks sounding like a firing squad. Besides, Big Pete's the type who might say something bad really nicely, quietly: 'Now, a little birdie tells me . . .' No one would hear a thing. The knocking has turned into the impatient hammering of a massive fist.

Eliot looks down at the slabbed pavement below. If he climbs onto the windowsill and then, holding on to the sill, dangles his long legs down the outside of the building so that he is hanging, he can drop down, and as he lands he will bend his knees to absorb the impact, and then he will run. He throws his legs over the sill. A key – Big Pete's master key – turns in the lock and the door swings open. Eliot is already letting go when Big Pete comes into the flat with a pair of yellow curtains over his arm.

Eliot's cigarette lands last, and softly.

The Papergirl

SHE WENT MISSING around the time I started my paper round. Nobody knew for sure what had happened to her, but there was speculation that she had just run away, as she had done before, and that she would come back eventually, still in one piece.

I was delivering the weekly free newspaper, which was half local news and half adverts. I carried a hundred papers in a luminous, waterproof bag that weighed me down on one side and I pictured the steady crushing of my spine.

Some people didn't want them, and put signs in their windows saying 'NO JUNK MAIL, NO FREE NEWSPAPERS'. There were latches to deal with, and dogs barking through doors and snarling through letter-boxes, and, at one house, a dog loose outside.

It was a big dog, already barking furiously as it tore around the side of the house. I was a long way from the gate, right out in the open. The dog, teeth bared, was on me in seconds, but I had turned away so that it only savaged the heavy-duty paper bag.

A man had appeared at the side of the house and was calling off the dog. I recognised him from Sunday school.

He called to me, 'Are you all right?'

'Yes, thank you,' I said. I was already walking away. I could hear the shake in my voice. I closed the gate behind me and walked on to the next house.

I had to do the farms as well. I didn't get extra for the long farm tracks; it was still a penny a paper.

The following week, when I reached the house of the Sunday school teacher and the savage dog, I just threw the newspaper over the gate. In American films, kids with paper rounds just threw the papers onto people's front lawns as they cycled by. I wondered if I'd get into trouble.

When I reached the crossroads, I crossed over and came back on the other side. From time to time, as I walked along, my fingers touched the side of my bag and I could feel the damage done by the dog. I thought about the girl who had still not turned up. She went to the same school as me, but she was in a different year and I didn't really know her. There were rumours going around that she'd gone to see a boy she met on holiday, or maybe she met him online. Everyone expected her, at any moment, to come back looking embarrassed.

As I approached the Sunday school teacher's house, but on the other side of the road, I saw what looked like so many little white birds lifting off the pavement and settling again. I saw them dragging along the ground and realised they were not birds but the newspaper, torn to pieces by the dog. The scraps were scattering in the wind, and the picture the front page carried was skittering away down the road.

Winter Closing

ON THE FROSTY lawn, beneath the naked birches, the winter perennials are blooming. The garden path, on which there was black ice this morning, has been salted to prevent the fracturing of wrists, the breaking of hips, the shattering of pelvises.

A breeze brings flurries of brittle leaves in through the open door of the old house. They skitter across the varnished floorboards and collect in the corners of the entrance hall and underneath the ticket desk. Sandra, handing change and leaflets to the ladies who came on the coach, shivers. Excusing herself, she gets up from behind the desk to go and close the front door, shutting out the wind if not the cold.

Sandra is only temporary. She is good with the visitors but does not like the house.

The ladies, waiting for their tour guide, browse the merchandise, leafing through posthumously published memoirs and picking up postcards – a grim portrait and an image of the house surrounded by an eerie, computer-generated mist.

Hearing footsteps in the corridor, the ladies turn to see

their tour guide coming into the entrance hall, wearing a cardigan over so many jumpers that his buttons strain. The smell of his lunchtime cigarette clings to him.

Derek does not smoke in the house. In his lunch hour, he has a cup of soup at the kitchen table and then goes out, walking down to the corner shop, in sunshine or the autumn winds, the recent rain and now the frost. He loves this old house but feels the need to escape for a short while when he can. The shopkeeper is cool towards Derek. She tells the other customers, 'He works at Mary's house,' and they put their money down on the counter so that they can leave. Perhaps the locals imagine that Derek brings something of the house with him, carrying it in his wake down the hill and into the shop. Perhaps they think he ought to stay put inside the house, inside the grounds, or even better just stay at home and leave the house to go to ruin.

Returning from the shop with dog food in a carrier bag, Derek smoked a cigarette on the back doorstep, blowing his smoke rings into the garden, gazing out at the towering leylandii, before coming inside to begin the afternoon tour.

Derek can see that Sandra is feeling the cold. The website advises visitors to wear their coats in the house whatever the season. Her predecessor never took off her coat, but Sandra's cagoule, which is hanging in the kitchen next to his own, would not keep out this chill. While Sandra extracts a scarf from her bag, Derek turns to his group, clapping his hands together like the schoolmaster he once was. The sound echoes around him. 'Good afternoon,' he says. 'I'm Derek and I will be your tour guide today.'

He introduces the ladies to the house, saying something about its history and pointing out its features. Moving on to the arrival of its most illustrious resident, he puts on the spectacles that he wears on a chain around his neck and reads from his copy of Mary's memoirs: '*Mother and I made the long journey by car in the middle of the night so that I would sleep all the way and not get travel sick. We arrived in the city at dawn. I opened my eyes and found myself in this ghastly and foul-smelling place.*' Looking up at the ladies, he adds, 'Despite this apparent hostility towards the city, Mary remained here as an adult and ended her days here.'

The attention of some, he notices, is wandering – some of the ladies are looking around at the closed doors; they are peering up the staircase towards the bedrooms.

'We'll start upstairs,' says Derek. 'Please follow me.'

He shepherds his group up the stairs and down to the far end of the landing. Opening the first of the two doors, he brings them into the smaller bedroom, in which there is nothing but a chest of empty drawers and a bare mattress on a single bed.

'This,' he says, 'was Mary's room when she was a child. It has been kept as it was when she died, by which time she was occupying the master bedroom.'

'So was this then a guest room?' asks one of the ladies.

'It was never used as one,' says Derek.

Someone asks about the patch of wallpaper behind the door, where the pattern has been picked at and peeled away. 'That's where Mary was made to stand,' says Derek, 'facing the wall, when she was disobedient.'

He leads them into the master bedroom, where the curtains are closed. Switching on the ceiling light, he says, 'Mary kept the curtains on this side of the house closed, believing that her neighbour watched her.' He takes his place at the head of the queen-size bed and straightens the corner of the lilac satin quilt. 'Mary was a creature of habit. She woke early and started her day with a glass of warm water with lemon for its cleansing effect. After taking a bath – we will see the bathroom in a moment – she ate a hot breakfast in the kitchen before beginning her day's writing.'

A lady says, 'Have you ever seen the ghost?'

'Oh yes,' says Derek. 'You might sense her presence around the house.'

The ladies agree that it certainly is dreadfully cold, and one in a fur-trimmed coat shudders dramatically. Someone, indicating a bedside photograph of a young man, asks, 'Was that her husband?'

'That's her father,' says Derek, 'who abandoned her in childhood.'

The ladies close in to get a better look at him.

'There were men who loved Mary,' says Derek, 'or thought they loved her, only until they got to know her. She was repeatedly rejected and disappointed by the men in her life. When she felt ill-treated, things could get nasty. She was often infatuated with unattainable men who must have seemed as if they could not hurt her.'

He moves the ladies out of the bedroom and down the landing to the bathroom. They admire the bath, which is the sort with feet, with claws.

When they return to the entrance hall, Sandra, wearing her scarf and hat and fingerless gloves, has the cash tin out and is counting the takings, eager to close up and get home.

There are no radiators in the house. The portable heater that Sandra keeps next to the ticket desk makes little difference. The house closes for the winter on the shortest day of the year, avoiding the enormous task of trying to heat it throughout the coldest months.

This is the last tour of the season. Derek would prefer to work through, but his proposal of a Christmas tour was not approved. Health and safety was mentioned. And Sandra, who has a family, would not want to do it anyway.

Derek ushers the ladies down the corridor and into the kitchen. Standing behind the solitary chair at the head of the farmhouse table, he conjures up the author breakfasting, the smell of percolating coffee, the scent of the garden coming in through an open window.

Lifting his spectacles again, he reads from Mary's memoirs: '*I liked to sit in the kitchen and feed the birds, putting bread on the windowsill, although my mother said that I must not because it was a sure way to attract mice and rats, and that I should not be bringing birds to the house, either, because they were crawling with disease, with lice. A sparrow landed on the sill and glanced into the kitchen with its small, bright eye and my mother struck it with her broom handle.*'

As they leave the kitchen, Derek notices some droppings. He knows that he ought to set traps for the mice but never does, not wanting to come back and find them trapped but not quite dead.

His ladies are chattering amongst themselves as he walks them back into the entrance hall. He pauses in front of a panelled wall and waits until he has their attention. Then, with the air of a magician who is about to perform a vanishing trick, he puts his hand on one of the panels and pushes so that a hidden door opens, letting them into the living room. The ladies think this is delightful.

As with the bedroom, the curtains are closed and he

leaves them that way, as Mary did, turning the light on instead. 'Mary hated this room,' he says. 'She spent hours in here as a child, studying an illustrated Bible and doing her piano practice. She and her mother rarely had visitors. This chair,' he says, indicating an armchair in the corner, 'was referred to as the guest chair, but it has perhaps never been used. Even at school, Mary found it hard to make friends.' He seeks out another page in Mary's memoirs and reads, '*The girls didn't like me and I didn't like them much, either. The boys were only after one thing and even the ones who seemed different let me down in the end.*' Looking up brightly, he says, 'She began, instead, to write.'

One lady, eyeing a typewriter on a desk in the corner, and the shelves of books above it, says, 'Did she write in here?'

'She did,' says Derek.

'But she hated this room.'

'Yes,' says Derek, 'she did. After breakfast, Mary would come in here. She wrote a thousand words a day, rarely stopping for lunch, having a bottle of wine opened instead. The maid would bring an evening meal – something cold, even in the winter, even at Christmas – to Mary's desk before leaving for the day. Mary died in the night and the maid found her here at her desk, her final supper untouched, except by the mice.'

'Are there mice?' says someone.

'It's an old house,' says Derek, 'full of holes.'

Over by the draughty fireplace, a lady's teeth chatter.

Derek speaks about Mary's commercial success and critical failure and the emotional impact of the lampooning of her later novels in particular, in which she increasingly punished her men for abandoning her heroines, for being disrespectful and unfaithful to the women who loved them. He indicates the newspapers piled high on the sofa, her hoard of negative reviews.

'At the same time, Mary was increasingly having difficulties with the locals.' He reads her account of the boys who bullied her: '*They come to the house day or night to put notes and burning and stinking things through my letterbox, stamping on my flowerbeds and breaking my windows. While I am working, and even in my sleep, I am on edge, listening for the clattering of my letterbox, the shattering of glass, anticipating the smell of burning. They run away, laughing.*

'She believed that the boys who lived next door were responsible, although she never caught them. She is suspected of retaliation, of setting fire to the boys' house. The youngest died in the blaze but Mary's guilt could not be proved. She continued to write until her death but was unable to find a publisher for her final works.'

'Have you read all her novels?' asks someone.

'Oh yes,' says Derek. 'I'm a huge fan.'

He directs the group back into the entrance hall, returning them to the ticket desk to purchase books and postcards, which forces Sandra to take her hands out of her pockets and open the cash tin again.

The minibus is waiting in the driveway, and the ladies go towards it in the last of the day's sunlight, careful on the path despite the salt.

Sandra follows Derek into the kitchen, where he switches on the kettle, takes coffee powder and milk powder out of the cupboard and makes them both a cup of coffee

– Sandra's in the mug she brings with her from home and takes away again at the end of the day, and his in one of the cups that belongs to the house. Sandra will not sit in Mary's chair and so she stands, complaining again about the cold, and Derek says, 'You get used to it.' He does not expect, though, that she will stay long enough to get used to it. None of them stays for long.

Derek, on the other hand, will never leave. 'It does get cold,' he agrees, 'but no wonder, a big old house like this, with its bare floorboards and single glazing.'

'And the ghost,' says Sandra, testing the heat of her coffee.

Derek looks at Sandra in surprise. 'There isn't a ghost,' he says. 'We say there's a ghost because that's what they want to hear. It's what they pay for.'

Sandra frowns and drinks her coffee quickly, rinses and dries her mug and puts it in her handbag. 'It's getting dark,' she says, reaching for her cagoule. 'Your wife will be wondering where you are.'

'I'm not married,' says Derek, taking the other cagoule down from its peg, 'but the dog will be waiting for his walk.'

They go together down the corridor and into the entrance hall. Derek holds the front door open but Sandra has stopped at the ticket desk. Fishing her keys out of her handbag, she says, 'I just have a few last things to do. You go. Have a nice Christmas.'

'You too,' says Derek, stepping outside. As he pulls the door to behind him, he hears Sandra singing so that she won't be frightened. He feeds his arm into the sleeve of his cagoule (it is awkwardly tight – too many jumpers, he thinks) and is on the path when he remembers his bag of dog food, and the Christmas card he meant to give to Sandra. He goes back inside, back across the entrance hall – Sandra has disappeared somewhere – and down the corridor, into the gloomy kitchen. Gathering up his things, he pauses to say, 'Merry Christmas, Mary.' A distant door opens or closes. Hearing Sandra singing, Derek hurries to catch her. By the time he comes into the entrance hall, though, she has gone. She has locked the front door behind her. It is only when Derek puts his hand into his pocket for his keys and instead finds a tissue, that he realises he is wearing Sandra's cagoule. He sees, briefly, through the window in the door, Sandra at the end of the garden path, walking away in his cagoule with his keys in the pocket. He knocks on the glass and then bangs with his fist on the door, but Sandra is already through the garden gate, lost behind the high hedge. 'Damn it,' he says to himself.

With the sun gone down and no lights on in the house, it has become hard to see. He goes back to the kitchen, banging his hip on the corner of the table as he crosses the room to the back door, but that is locked too, as are the windows, and the keys are on the same ring as his front door key.

He will have to wait for the cleaner to come. She can let him out when she arrives and he can go home to his hungry dog. He hopes he will not have to wait too long.

He goes to turn on the light, but nothing happens – the bulb must have gone. Still, he can see well enough to put the kettle on. He opens the cupboard in which he keeps his powdered soups but there are none left in the packet. There is only the coffee powder and milk powder. He puts a spoonful of each in a cup, then sits down and lights a cigarette, blowing smoke rings across the long pine table.

It occurs to him that the kettle is not boiling. He stands in front of it flicking the switch but it is dead. He tries a light switch in the corridor and then one in the entrance hall but nothing works. He thinks at first that there must have been a power cut, before remembering that Sandra will have been instructed to turn it off at the mains for the winter, to prevent electrical failure, an unwanted fire. The mains switch is in a cupboard behind the ticket desk, but even before he tries the cupboard door he knows that it will be locked.

He looks at his watch. Does the cleaner come in the evening, he wonders, or in the morning? He does not want to have to spend the night here. He does not want to sleep in Mary's bed, or in the inhospitable guest bedroom.

His shoes are loud in the entrance hall as he strides towards the living room, in which, on the desk on the far side of the room, there is a telephone. Holding open the door in the panelling, letting in what moonlight he can, he looks into the room. Leaving the door ajar, he feels his way to the desk. He picks up and holds to his ear the receiver of this phone that has long since been disconnected. 'Oh,' he says to himself, listening to the dead line, 'of course.'

Replacing the receiver, he stands for a moment. He does not have a mobile phone. Sandra has one but it is not in the pocket of her cagoule.

Back in the entrance hall, Derek kneels down by the front door and shouts through the letterbox. In his little house, if he shouted through the letterbox or banged on a wall, someone would probably respond, but in this house with its long driveway and its big garden, no one hears him or at least no one comes.

When his knees begin to seize up, he stands. He has never met the cleaner. He knows she exists because when he arrives each morning the floors have been swept and mopped. The house does not clean itself. He will wait another hour and if she hasn't come he will think of something else. He could break the windows, but that would be a last resort. My God, he thinks, it's unbearably cold. His extremities are like ice. He'll need some warmth while he waits. He returns to the living room and stands in the doorway, looking across the room at the fireplace. He knows that the chimney has not been blocked up, but there is no fuel. The ticket desk has been cleared, the flammable merchandise locked away inside the cupboard. His gaze falls on the contents of the shelves above the desk – a lifetime's work, Mary's oeuvre. He could burn a few of the more recent, unpopular ones. He does not like to do it but the books are not irreplaceable, nor very valuable. They sell for change in charity shops. There are also the newspapers, but they would be more difficult to replace.

He moves into the room, but when he reaches Mary's desk the door clicks shuts behind him, leaving him in darkness. He fumbles for his matches. He has Sandra's song in his head. He tries to sing it but he cannot carry the tune. Striking a match, he holds the shivering flame out in front of him like a blazing torch and, by its light, reaches out to take from the lower shelf a couple of five-hundred-page paperbacks. 'Sorry, Mary,' he says. He edges over to the hearth and places them on the grate. Then, squatting in front of them, he puts his little flame to the books. The paper browns at the edges but he cannot get it to stay alight. He tears out the pages, screws them up and lights another match but still has no success. The newspapers then, he thinks. He moves a stack from the sofa to the hearth, selects the uppermost paper and crushes it into the fireplace, stabbing it down with the poker. When he strikes another match and puts it to the newspaper, the blaze is so sudden that his fingers are hurt, and there is a fury in the fire that you might expect from petrol. He shifts backwards, away from the noxious smoke, but the flames come too, spewing from the fireplace and igniting the rest of the stack.

Derek looks around in alarm for something to keep this from becoming an inferno. There is no rug on the floorboards, no big blanket on the sofa. He needs the fire extinguisher that is in the entrance hall, underneath the emergency exit sign, the arrow pointing towards the front door, the little white stick man running for his life.

Derek makes his way towards the far wall, feeling around for the door, the secret crack in the panelling. When he touches the adjoining wall, he moves his hands back the other way, and then back again, but he can't for the life of him find it. 'Where's the door?' he asks, scraping at the wood with his fingernails, like a man buried alive.

He will have to break a window after all. Retrieving the poker, he goes to the curtains and pulls them aside. An unexpected darkness seems to press up against the glass. Choosing a pane, he smashes it and is surprised to find, on the other side, a thick wall of leylandii. He does not remember it growing so close to the house. The hedge grew thick, certainly, and tall, but it is right up against the house, against the windows, and now that this pane is broken, the branches are pushing through into the living room. There is no gap big enough for him to climb through. He smashes another pane but the same is true there – he finds only an impenetrable wall of trunks and branches pressing in through the window, while, behind him, the fire burns the piano, the music books, the children's Bible.

He tries to break the branches but he can't. He fills his bleeding hands with nothing more than twigs. Dropping this kindling at his feet, he yanks down the curtains, throwing them over the flames, but the material just burns. In the smoke-filled room, Derek is seized by a fit of coughing. Pulling his cardigan up over his mouth and his nose, he retreats to the corner. He will look, again, for the door; it is inconceivable that he will not be able to find it. Standing in the corner in his jumpers, turning his back to the burning room, he thinks to himself, as the fire roars, how cold it still is.

Point of Entry

WE STAND IN the kitchen, looking at the broken glass on the windowsill and on the worktop and in the sink. I reach for Rosie's hand.

It is lunchtime but we are still in our pyjamas and dressing gowns. We have put on our shoes so that any glass we can't see on the floor will not cut our feet.

The police have been and gone, leaving us with a crime number. On the worktop, surrounded by the hundreds of tiny silica balls that have spilt from the double glazing, from the metal bar that keeps the panes apart, is my glass fruit bowl.

'My fruit bowl's been chipped,' I say, reaching for it.

'Never mind,' says Rosie. 'You should leave it there,' she adds, 'until the man from Forensics has been.'

I see a shard of glass in the toaster and hear the doorbell ring.

'That will be him,' says Rosie, letting go of my hand as both of us turn and look down the hallway towards the dark shape of a man at the front door, his outline fragmented by the patterned glass. She goes to let him in.

Stepping onto the doormat, wiping his big work boots,

he tells us his name. It is taped, as well, to the side of his heavy-duty metallic case – TOBY CARSON – in big black capital letters.

Rosie closes the door behind him and introduces herself. 'And that's Laura,' she says, glancing towards where I am standing in the kitchen doorway.

I offer coffee, which Toby, coming into the kitchen and putting his case down on the floor, declines. I start to make it anyway, for Rosie and me. I make a move towards the kettle but it is in front of the window and is probably not to be touched, and it no doubt has glass in it anyway. Instead, I take a saucepan out of the cupboard, hesitate near the sink and then take the pan upstairs, filling it from the bath tap.

When I come back down, Toby is in the garden with Rosie, looking at the point of entry from the other side. I can hear their conversation through the empty window frame. He is showing her where a screwdriver has been used and where the broken bits of window have been thrown onto the lawn so as to land silently. He uses the passive tense, as if these things have just happened and no one is to blame.

They come back inside. 'I can see that gloves were worn,' he says, knowing this just by looking. Of the silica balls that roll around on the worktop, he says, 'You'll be finding these for weeks.'

The water is boiling on the hob. I take it off and make coffee for two, moving awkwardly around the kitchen, getting in the way.

'Was entry deep into the house?' says Toby.

'They went into the living room,' says Rosie, taking him through. I follow behind. She shows him the desk through which someone has rifled, the bottom drawer from which her holiday money has been taken. Toby crouches down and opens the drawer. 'You'd hardly know anyone had been in here,' says Rosie. 'They've not made a mess. But my euros have gone.' She tells him how it feels to know that someone was creeping around down here while she was asleep upstairs.

'At least you're all right,' he says, standing again, six foot in his work boots, and Rosie smiles up at him.

We go back into the kitchen and Toby opens his silvery case. It is lined with thick foam with holes cut out for all his equipment, everything fitting somewhere. Using a brush like a make-up brush, he dusts fine powder over the broken glass. Working on a sizeable shard from the sill, he says, 'We've got a bootprint here.'

While he lifts the print, he tells us about the bootprint database. 'That's interesting,' says Rosie. He tells us about the matching-up of wear and tear on the sole. 'That's clever,' she says. His police radio crackles.

Toby takes his equipment through to the living room where he finds fingermarks in the dust, but no prints. He puts his equipment away and closes his case. 'I've got your number,' he says.

'I'll have to get some more euros,' says Rosie.

'Are you going somewhere nice?' asks Toby.

'Rome,' she says.

'Lovely,' he says. 'I love Rome.'

They smile at one another and then Toby leaves, carrying the bootprint in his heavy-duty case. Rosie lingers on the doorstep, watching him as he walks away, as he gets into his Scientific Support van and drives off down the road.

She closes the back door but the cold air still comes in through the hole in the side of our house, just as it has been coming in all morning. I shiver and Rosie says, 'Are you cold?'

We'd become running partners in our first week at university, running together throughout the autumn term. On our first winter run, we came to a stop near our halls of residence, by the pond, which had frozen over. We stood with our hands on our knees, breathing hard. Rosie, the first to recover, touched her foot to the ice, testing her weight, stepping out.

'It might break,' I said.

She walked out into the middle before turning to face me. 'Come on,' she said.

Stepping cautiously onto the frozen surface, I remained at the edge. 'It's getting dark,' I said. Rosie waited for me, and in the end I took small steps towards her.

'Are you cold?' she said. She reached for me, taking my hand. Surprised by my icy fingertips, she said, 'You'll get chilblains.' She squeezed my hand between hers as if she were pressing flowers. She blew on my frozen fingertips and my blood began flowing again; my fingertips started to throb. My other hand, which was not being held, remained numb at my side. 'Better?' she asked.

'Yes,' I said.

She dropped her gaze, looking at my lips, which were dry, which had been salved but were cracking at the corners. My fingertips were hurting. I was looking away, listening for the creaking of ice beneath us, when she kissed me.

'We lock our doors,' I say. 'We lock our windows.'

Rosie nods.

'We could get laminated glass in the replacement window, to stop anyone else getting in that way.'

She shrugs. 'If you like,' she says.

She goes upstairs for a shower and I clean up. I put the pieces of glass into the bin. I sweep the worktop, the silica balls scattering and getting into the gaps. I sweep the floor.

When I have finished, I sit down at the kitchen table and see, near my foot, a small fragment that I have missed.

On the table, next to our crime number, two mugs of lukewarm coffee sit untouched. I reach for mine and wait for the man who is coming to board up the window through which our morning sun comes in.

The Sketch

AILSA MOVED INTO the light. She held the drawing close to the bedroom window and studied it. She had found it inside her old portfolio case, which she had opened today for the first time since her youth. The rest of the work – a collection of self-portraits and still lifes – was familiar, recognisable as her own, but *this* piece – she would swear on the Bible – she had never seen before, not until just a minute ago when she had turned over an unfinished head and found this strange thing underneath.

As a girl, she'd had her heart set on art school, on nothing less than the Slade; she had hoped to become an artist, perhaps an illustrator. In the event, further education had not been a possibility, due to her mother's illness. 'You can get that idea out of your head,' her father had told her. The portfolio had been put away then and had not been opened again while her father was alive, although Ailsa had taken it with her when she married Peter, and again when they moved out of their first house and into this flat. She was supposed to have thrown things out *before* the move, but she had been finding it hard. In the end, she had brought much of it with her, promising Peter that she would, when she'd had a chance to think about it, keep only what was absolutely necessary; she would be brutal.

Now the portfolio lay unzipped and wide open on the unmade bed. The drawing's heavy pencil lines captured the likeness of some kind of troll or sprite, some kind of devilish-looking creature. This was not something *she* had drawn, surely. Her own work had been much more conventional. She did not remember making this picture; it did not look like her work. She touched it, as if she might be able to feel those textures suggested by the pencil lines: the roughness, the hairiness. When she looked very closely, at details rather than at the whole thing in one go, perhaps there *was* something familiar about it; and whether or not it had come out of her, it did speak to her in some way.

The graphite had come away on her fingers; her fingerprints made an ellipsis at the edge of the paper.

Her father's funeral took place on a Wednesday. Peter told her he couldn't go because he had to work, and that he would need the car. He did not like her to drive it anyway: she had once scraped a wing, scratched the paintwork, and she had a bad habit of letting the windscreen washer reservoir run dry. He accused her of not looking after it properly. Ailsa thought he was being unfair: in recent years, she had taken a car maintenance class for beginners, and she had been a good student – she had paid attention and made careful notes, which she kept in order in a ring binder. On the other hand, it was true that she was sometimes careless with that old car of his.

She caught the bus to the crematorium, with the baby strapped to her chest. It was a cold midwinter day, but fresh and rather lovely, and as she walked through the gates of the crematorium the sun emerged briefly.

She sat at the front, and as the curtains closed around the coffin a distant relative leaned close, laid a hand on Ailsa's and said, as if to soothe her, though she was not crying, 'That's just his body going. He doesn't want it any more. He's free now.' Ailsa looked at the relative's hand pressing down on her own; it looked like her father's.

'Out,' said Peter. He reached back into the cardboard box. 'Out.' The discard pile in the flat's narrow hallway reminded Ailsa of the bonfires they used to have in their back garden when she was little. She always made a Guy to put on top of it, with an old pillowcase for a face and her mother's tights for limbs, all stuffed with her father's newspaper. Her father, approaching the bonfire with a box of matches, said that if any hedgehogs were hibernating in there they'd better get out now, and then he lit the twists of paper he'd screwed into the gaps, and Ailsa watched the Guy. She imagined, as the flames rose higher, the Guy's felt-tipped face turning towards her, seeking her out in the dark, in the firelight, its overlong limbs twitching and shifting away from the heat. Then the nylon and the paper would catch and the Guy would flare and – so soon, so quickly, considering the time and care that had been put into making him – be gone, apart from the fragments that, still burning, blew towards her, and she had to step back so that she would not get holes in her winter coat.

'Keep,' said Peter, putting aside the canvas of tiny handprints and footprints, done when Bella was only a few weeks old.

'Out,' said Peter. He was holding Ailsa's portfolio. It had not sounded like a question, but Ailsa said, as she came forward and took the portfolio from his hands, 'I'm not sure.'

'You can't hang on to all this stuff,' he said. 'We don't have space for it here.'

'I don't see how we're going to manage in this little flat,' said Ailsa. 'Not with the baby.'

'We have no choice,' said Peter. 'You know that. We have to downsize.'

'All my drawings are in here,' she said.

'But what would you need to keep them for?' asked Peter.

'I might want to look at them,' said Ailsa.

Peter, delving back into the box, adding sheaves of old paperwork to the pile, said, 'You haven't looked at them in twenty years.'

'I looked at them yesterday,' said Ailsa. 'There was one drawing in there that I don't even remember doing. It's nothing like the others. It's peculiar, rather horrid, but I think in a way it's better – more vivid and realistic and affecting – than anything else I've done. It looked like if I touched it, I'd be able to feel the textures – dirty hair and stubble and ragged nails. And its eyes look right back at you, I swear they do. I'm going to show you.' She went to the kitchen table, moving the baby's things to make space for her portfolio. She opened it up. 'It's here,' she said, 'in amongst the self-portraits, just under these heads.'

Peter came and stood at her shoulder, waiting.

'It's here,' she said again, 'somewhere . . .'

'Ailsa,' said Peter.

She rummaged through the sheets of paper, going all

the way down to the bottom of the pile. 'It was . . .'

'Ailsa,' said Peter. 'We're all having to make sacrifices. Even Bella is having to make sacrifices. She'll have to manage with less stuff, less space, no garden.'

Ailsa looked at Bella, who everyone said had her eyes, but the baby's eyes were blue while Ailsa's were dark. Perhaps the baby's eyes would change; Ailsa expected that they would, in due course. Bella was still so young – too young, Ailsa thought, to even see her across a room, to see anything more than a murky blur where Ailsa was standing.

The picture of the troll, the sprite – the devilish-looking whatever-it-was – was not there. She would swear that she had put it back inside the portfolio, but now it was gone. In between the heads and the fruit, she found a sheet of paper that was blank except for the fingerprints at the edge, one so clear that you could see the pattern, like ripples in water. She tried to match it to her own. The others were just smudges.

Ailsa saw Peter's face contort; she watched him spit his tea back into his mug. Holding it at a distance, he said, 'Is there *salt* in this?'

'There shouldn't be,' she said.

'I know there *shouldn't* be,' he said, 'but *is* there?'

'Mine's fine,' said Ailsa, but she did not take sugar anyway; she drank her tea black, with lemon. 'Perhaps the sugar and salt got mixed up during the move.'

'And the mug's dirty,' complained Peter, putting it down heavily and pushing himself away from the kitchen table. Ailsa looked and saw that the mug was indeed dirty: there was a smudge on the side, just where it said BEST DAD.

She wondered who had bought that mug. *She* had not bought it for him, and of course the baby had not; had he bought it for himself? As a joke, perhaps.

When she had cleared the breakfast table and given Bella her milk, she went to look for her portfolio. She had to make some decisions today; she had to decide which of her belongings to keep and which to discard. She called to Peter, 'Where's my portfolio?'

'I put it out,' said Peter.

Ailsa looked at the pile that remained in the hallway. 'Out where?'

'I put it out for the dustmen,' said Peter.

Still in her dressing gown, Ailsa hurried out of the flat and down the stairs. At the bottom, she pushed open the front door. The world was bitterly cold.

The bins had been emptied. Ailsa heard the distant screech of the bin lorry.

There was a lot of work to be done on the flat, to make it habitable. The kitchen in particular was disgusting. Ailsa remembered her mother saying that the kitchen was the most important room in a home; the kitchen was its heart.

Ailsa sat the baby in a rocker in the doorway and set to tearing up the old lino, which she despised – it looked like a vast and foul chessboard. She was halfway through the task before it struck her that the tiles revealed beneath were just the same as they'd had at home when she was young. For a moment, looking at these childhood tiles, it was as if it might be possible to go back and start over again, make a fresh start, have another go. Then she saw the dirty marks on the doorframe, and she thought of her father, home from the workshop, slouching in the doorway, a small man with grime on his hands, in the whorls of his skin, oil under his fingernails.

When Peter came home from work, he stopped in the kitchen doorway and looked at her. Looking back at him with red-rimmed eyes, she told him, 'I don't want to live here,' but her voice seemed thin, whispery, and she was not sure he heard her.

'You're a state,' he said. 'Some women are like this after having a baby.' He reached down and lifted Bella out of the rocker. 'Sssh . . .' he said to her. 'Sssh . . .' To Ailsa, he said, 'Do you think you should see a doctor?'

Ailsa was often woken at night by Peter's snoring, which crescendoed until his breathing stopped altogether, before starting again. But this was different: Ailsa had woken to find Peter lying there with his hands around his own throat; she had been woken by the choking noises he was making. His eyes – she saw, as she got herself up onto her elbows to see what was going on – were very wide. As she turned on the bedside lamp, he finally managed to draw in a breath, a desperate, shallow gulp of air, and then another. When he could speak again, he whispered, 'I couldn't breathe.'

'I expect it's this flat,' she said. 'All the old dirt and dust has got into your lungs.'

'It felt like something was sitting on my chest,' he said.

In the lamplight, Ailsa looked at his chest, but the T-shirt that he wore in bed was black – there was no evidence that anything had been there; she could see no telltale marks.

When it happened again, she said to him, 'Do you think you should see a doctor?'

◊

The doctor found nothing wrong. 'He says I'm in good shape,' said Peter.

Ailsa washed the T-shirt. She spring-cleaned the flat, with the windows wide open, even though it was winter. When she found grimy streaks low down on walls that she knew she had cleaned, she supposed that they might just be scuff marks from Peter's polished shoes. When she found the same marks down near the bottom of the baby's bedroom door, she began to get up in the night whether or not she could hear Bella crying; a silence was more worrying. Every few hours she was out in the hallway, going into Bella's room, turning on the overhead light to look for grubby prints on the bedding or on the babygro or on Panda, who had been Ailsa's own favourite cuddly toy when she was small.

'I've been moving the furniture,' said Ailsa.

'I can see that,' said Peter. He stood in the doorway of the baby's room, blocking the light from the hallway, the toes of his shoes on Bella's carpet. 'But—' He looked at the thigh-high wall of furniture that Ailsa had built around the cot, inside which the baby lay prone. 'But whatever for?' said Peter. 'Bella can't even sit up yet, let alone climb out of her cot.'

'It's not to keep Bella *in*,' said Ailsa.

'Then what?' said Peter, but Ailsa did not reply; she was busy lashing the piano stool to the fireguard. These were both things that were not supposed to have come with them to the flat: they had no fireplace here, and no space for the piano, and even if there had been space they would not have been able to get it up all the stairs. The piano had belonged to Ailsa's mother, whose repertoire of fey little tunes had never seemed to make use of the lower notes. For equilibrium, Ailsa had made a point of only ever playing the lower notes, until her mother complained, after which Ailsa was forbidden to touch the piano at all. Nonetheless, the piano had come to her when her father went into the home, and then Peter had got rid of it because it would not fit into the flat.

When Peter had arrived home from the bank with the news that they would have to move out of their house and into this flat, the piano had been Ailsa's first concern. She objected to its loss. She told him that when she was a child she had loved the piano; she had longed to touch its forbidden keys. Peter agreed that it was good for a child to learn a musical instrument, but said that Bella would just have to learn something smaller, like the flute. 'It doesn't really matter,' said Peter. 'It just has to be something small.'

Peter stepped into the baby's room now, coming closer to the wall that Ailsa had built around the cot. 'How are we supposed to get to Bella?' he asked.

Ailsa straightened up. 'I can climb over it,' she said. 'I'm tall enough.'

Peter made an appointment at the surgery for Ailsa, and dropped her off on his way to work. When the mid-afternoon bus brought her back, she saw – as she made her way from the bus stop on the corner, with the baby in a sling – the furniture out on the street, and Peter opening the boot of his car. He picked up the piano stool and put it in. As Ailsa walked past him, he picked up the fireguard.

Still in her coat, still bearing the baby, she stood looking into Bella's room. She went back out to where Peter was busy fitting everything into the back of his car. As Peter slammed the boot down, Ailsa said to him, 'What have you done?'

'I've taken all that crap out of Bella's room,' said Peter.

'I can see that,' said Ailsa. 'But whatever for?'

'I'm taking it to the tip,' said Peter. He checked that the boot was secure and moved towards the front of the car. 'What did the doctor say?' he asked.

'I need more fresh air and exercise,' said Ailsa. 'And a hobby.'

'A hobby?' said Peter.

'A hobby,' said Ailsa. 'You know, like drawing. I might find a class to go to, pick up the still life again. Or perhaps not still life. I'm tempted to experiment, to try for that texture again. That hair was so realistic.'

'Are you still going on about that bloody sketch?' said Peter.

Sketch. She disliked the word. Sketch, like scratch, like retch, like etch. *Would you like to come and see my etchings?* A man – a friend of her father's – had actually said this to her once, a long time ago, and she had gone with him, this man she had known only slightly; she had actually gone with him to see his etchings, sketchings, scratchings, retchings, and she should not have done. Her father, when she got home, shaking and tearful, and told him, had looked at her, looked her up and down. 'Well, what did you expect,' he said, 'going home with him, and dressed like that?' And then, within the week, this friend of her father's was at their door, coming into the kitchen and joining them at their table as if nothing had happened, as if his being there – at their kitchen table with his fingers on their crockery – were in no way extraordinary.

'Why don't you decorate the baby's bedroom?' suggested Peter. 'It could do with brightening up. There's plenty for you to do here. You don't need to go out to a class. Find a hobby you can do at home.'

She had also liked reading, but since the baby had come along she had not so much as picked up a book, with the exception of baby books. Bella's books had no words in them, just stark black-and-white patterns.

At some point during her mother's illness, her father's friend – whose name Ailsa could barely recall now, whose name she had no desire to bring to mind – came to live with them for a while. When he sat with the family in their living room, Ailsa made sure always to have a book in front of her, one that was many hundreds of pages thick, the thickness of a door, or a thousand pages thick, the thickness of a wall. She learnt how to be in his company for hours at a time, day after day, and hardly see him. But at the same time, he had learnt how to get around her, for example by challenging her to a game – he would go to the games cupboard and make a show of choosing something, and her father would insist that their guest be indulged. When Ailsa went up to bed and closed her door, she wedged a chair under the handle before turning out the light. One morning, she threw out his shoes. Now she saw that this had been topsy-turvy thinking, as if throwing out his shoes could make him leave. Anyway, by the end of the day, the shoes were back in their place on the shoe rack and nothing was said, and she began to wonder if she had really done it at all or only thought about it.

Peter got into the driver's seat and slammed the door, and Ailsa stood and watched as he struggled with the engine. When he finally got it started, he pulled away angrily, leaving filthy exhaust fumes clouding the air. The car looked like a wreck but it could still get up speed on an open road, especially when Peter was cross and put his foot down too hard.

By the time Peter returned, Ailsa was sweeping the hallway with a dustpan and brush.

'What's that?' asked Peter, pointing at the baby's bedroom door.

'It's a padlock,' said Ailsa.

Peter opened his mouth; he shook his head. He followed Ailsa into the kitchen, watched her as she emptied the dustpan into the bin beneath the sink and put the dustpan and brush away in the cupboard. She undid the locket around her neck, with her mother in one half and her father in the other, both of them in black and white; she threaded the padlock key onto the chain and returned the locket to its place around her neck.

'This has to stop,' said Peter.

'Yes,' said Ailsa, looking up at the ceiling, at the grubby marks around the light fitting.

When Ailsa had put the baby to bed and locked the bedroom door, she ran herself a bubble bath and then went to bed herself. She felt terribly tired and yet found it difficult to settle and slept lightly until she was woken by an eerie quiet.

She got out of bed and went into the hallway. At the baby's door, she had to bend down so that the key on the chain around her neck could reach the lock. As she entered Bella's room, she snapped on the overhead light, so that nothing could hide in the dark; nothing, she thought, could sneak unseen beneath the furniture.

She approached the sleeping baby, and saw – in spite of the lock – filth on the bars of the cot. She carried the baby to the chair in the corner of the room and sat awake all night while Bella slept in her arms.

Peter found her there in the morning, with the bulb still burning. 'What are you doing there?' he asked. 'How long have you been sitting there? You look awful, Ailsa, absolutely awful.'

'This is your fault,' she whispered. The baby stirred on her chest. 'He's out and I can't put him back – there's nowhere for him to go back to.'

'What are you talking about?' asked Peter.

'The portfolio,' hissed Ailsa. 'I needed that portfolio but you threw it out.'

'I haven't got time for this,' said Peter. 'I've got work.' He went into the kitchen and ate a bowl of cereal standing up in front of the fridge. It was still dark outside when he left. The door slammed behind him.

Every morning, Peter drove north for twenty miles, and every evening he drove south again. Ailsa thought he drove too fast, always a little bit faster than the road allowed, overtaking everyone else as if he had more of a right to the road than they did. He would arrive home in a temper, fuming over some bad driver, some cyclist, always something, something that wasn't his fault, fuming at Ailsa as if it were *her* fault, as if *she* had cut him up, as if *she* had overlooked his right of way.

Ailsa washed the dishes and wiped the table, scrubbing at a stubborn stain that had got into the grain of the wood. She looked for the place mats. Peter disliked them – he thought them feminine – but they protected the table. She found them in the pile in the hallway; and right at the bottom, in the middle, just where she imagined the hedgehogs used to hide in the bonfire, Ailsa found the grey ring binder that she had used for evening classes in the years between her father going into the home and the baby being born. She sat and leafed through it, singing a tune that she'd learnt to play on the piano a long time ago.

'It's not too late,' said Ailsa. 'We can explain to the people in the house that we want it back, that the flat is too small for us, that we miss our garden. We can't possibly be happy here.'

Peter, taking off his shoes, said, 'But we can't afford the house any more.'

'There might be some money though,' said Ailsa. 'He might have left me something in his will.'

'And he might not have done,' said Peter. 'There might have been nothing left to leave. The home might have sucked him dry.'

Ailsa looked at Bella playing with her toys in the narrow hallway. 'But the flat is just too small,' she said, 'for the two of us and a baby.'

'Bella hardly counts,' said Peter. 'She's only little.'

'For now,' said Ailsa. 'But she's going to grow. She'll grow big. She'll be a young woman with size six feet and a will of her own.'

Peter looked down at Bella. He said to her, 'Is my baby going to have size six feet? Is she? Is she? I don't think so! No, I don't think so! Daddy loves her little feet! Little itsy bitsy feet! Yes, he does!'

'He keeps interfering with things,' said Ailsa.

'Who does?' asked Peter.

Ailsa did not know what to call him, and she'd rather avoid naming him anyway, for fear that it would somehow make him more real. But he was real enough: he'd been tampering, so that things that had worked when they'd first moved in had become temperamental or had broken down altogether. First the boiler had gone, and then the television: while Peter was down at the pub, getting to know the locals, Ailsa sat down to watch something and the screen went black. He tampered with the electrics, so that sometimes the lights did not work and she had to make do with what little daylight came in through the mean windows. And she kept finding – down at knee-height and underneath things and in tight corners that she had to peer at with a torch – those sooty streaks, those grey-black smears. The thought got into her head that if those dirty marks appeared on Panda's black limbs, she would not be able to see them. She put Panda into the wash, just to be sure that all the baby's things were clean.

He was just concerned about her, he said; she could do with a little rest, a few days without Bella to take care of. His mum would have her for the weekend; it was all arranged. In the morning, she should pack a bag of baby things, and when he got back from work he would drive Bella over to his mother's.

'But your mother's flat is even smaller than this one,' said Ailsa. 'She only has one bedroom.'

'Mum will manage just fine,' said Peter.

'But Bella needs more space,' said Ailsa.

'Perhaps,' said Peter, 'while Bella's at Mum's, you could go and see the doctor again.'

At night, while Ailsa slept ever more lightly and woke ever more frequently, Peter slept soundly, unless his own snoring or struggling to breathe woke him up. Only Ailsa was ever up and about in the night, in the baby's room, or sometimes out at the front of the flats, in between the flats and the road, looking at the moon or at a moonless sky, or at one of the very few people walking by, or at the cars that zipped past, and at their own car parked by the kerb. She stood there smoking the roll-ups that she was not supposed to have any more because of the baby, but which she liked because they cleared her head, they helped her to think.

She did not like to think of Bella going to Peter's mother's cramped and painfully quiet little flat. She did not want Peter taking Bella out in that crappy old car, driving so fast. With Bella here, in her own room, Ailsa could keep checking for smudgy marks on Bella's clothes or on her bedding. She considered the car, thinking of the engine, the underside, the parts that were already grimy, oily; how would one ever notice some small smudgy fingerprints on a vital part, such as a brake cable? If something were to happen, it might be impossible to say exactly how it had occurred.

◊

In the morning, at breakfast, Peter commented on the dark smudges under Ailsa's eyes. 'Did you sleep?' he asked.

'A bit,' said Ailsa. Although she had been up for most of the night, she had slept quite well in the final few hours.

Peter finished his cereal, put his bowl down near the sink and said, 'I'll be back after lunch to take Bella to Mum's. Get her bag ready. Remember to put in her formula.'

Ailsa nodded. She listened to Peter closing the door behind him. She stood and went to the window and looked down at him getting into his car and driving away. She watched him accelerating into the gloom, heading for the bypass.

She did not hurry to pack up the baby's things. Instead, while Bella sat in her high chair playing with her first solid food, Ailsa sat down and lit a roll-up. The charcoal-grey ring binder was still out on the kitchen table. The pages of careful notes and neat diagrams from the car maintenance class were dirty at the edges. It could go out for the dustmen now.

When her roll-up had almost burnt down to her grubby fingertips, she used the smoldering end to light another one. She might have all day now to sit and think about what to do next.

A Month of Sundays

RALPH HAD PLANNED to arrive with plenty of time in hand, but when he finally made it through the centre of town and pulled up alongside all the other cars in the car park, he saw that everyone else was already there, and indeed they had started going in through the crematorium's big wooden doors.

He climbed out of his Beetle and made his way across the gravel car park. It was like walking on sand or in deep snow; with every step, he sank a little way into the ground. He eyed a crow that was perched on a fence post, and it eyed him back.

Slipping into a pew at the back of the chapel, Ralph looked around for a familiar face, though he didn't know who he was hoping to see. He had even wondered if he might be the only one there, a lone figure in the pews. He had never met Brendan's daughter, who lived abroad. He had known Brendan's friends of course, because they had also been Ralph's friends, but there weren't any left. The rest of the lads had 'gone on ahead', according to Brendan, but Ralph did not believe in an afterlife. This, he thought, the here and now, was all there was. What would comfort him, in the time he had left, was having his memories to look back on. He hoped he had enough. It was like shopping before a bank holiday weekend – you had to make sure you had plenty of bread, plenty of milk, or you'd go hungry; you'd not be able to have that warming cup of tea you wanted.

They had said their goodbyes to their friends right here, at this same crematorium. Knowing the place so well, Ralph really should not have been late. He had not been delayed leaving home that morning, and other than having to negotiate the new one-way system, there had been no major incidents en route. Somehow, though, in the end, he had cut it fine. He did wonder if there was something subconscious in his arriving late, almost too late, because he hadn't really wanted to be here at all, at the funeral of his last living friend, his last friend full stop. Perhaps he had dawdled over his morning coffee without realising, or perhaps it was just that his car, which he'd had since it was brand new in the sixties, was on its last legs. The petrol gauge was broken so that there was always a danger of running out of fuel in the middle of even the shortest journey if the tank was not kept topped up. One of these days it would shudder to a stop and never start again. There seemed little point trading it in now though; it might see him through. On the other hand, he sometimes wondered if he should just say, 'What the hell,' and get himself something new; something for daytrips while the summer lasted, had he anyone to go with; something less draughty for the winter.

Even the dashboard clock was broken. Not that he needed it. His wristwatch was at the jeweller's for mending, but there was still the alarm clock on his bedside table, the carriage clock on the living room mantelpiece, digital displays on the cooker, the microwave, the central heating control panel, the phone. He was rarely unaware of the passing of time, the hour of the day. Even when he was out and about, he had his mobile phone for timekeeping. He had his phone in his coat pocket right now but hadn't looked at it since leaving the house. He'd had the radio on and, come to think of it, the schedule had not suggested that he was running late – Ken Bruce had still been on. He took his phone out of his pocket, so as to mute it, and saw that he was not late after all; he had, in fact, arrived quite a bit earlier than he had intended to. He looked around the packed room. Many people were reading the order of service. There was an order of service on the seat beside him but it wasn't the right one; it wasn't Brendan's. The elderly lady pictured on the front was all smiles, with a glass of sherry in her hand and a Christmas tree behind her. It was possible, Ralph supposed, that it had been left behind after the previous funeral, but really, at that moment, he understood what had happened. He began to get to his feet, but just then the music changed; the coffin was coming in. He sat down again.

Twenty-five minutes later, Ralph was exiting the chapel with everyone else, shaking the minster's hand on his way out, thanking him for the lovely service. He drifted into the garden and looked at the bouquets of flowers laid out on the slabs. He stooped to read the little cards attached to them.

'How did you know Kathleen?'

Ralph looked up at the woman who had asked him the

question, who was not someone he knew, and not someone he was likely to see again. Straightening up, he said to her, with a twinkle in his eye and in a conspiratorial tone, 'We were sweethearts.'

The woman looked shocked, and stepped forward eagerly. 'I thought there'd only ever been Bill,' she said. 'So you were before Bill? Or . . .'

Ralph nodded and gazed down at the flowers.

A younger woman came over, saying, 'Hello Susan,' and, holding out a hand to Ralph, 'I don't think we've met?'

'I'm Ralph,' he said, taking her hand.

'Ralph . . .' she said, trying to place him.

'A friend of your mother's,' said Susan, diplomatically.

'She might not have mentioned me,' said Ralph.

'This is Kathleen's daughter, Elaine,' said Susan.

'Of course,' said Ralph. 'You're the spitting image of your mother.' He could feel Susan studying the two of them, looking for the slightest resemblance.

'Are you local?' asked Elaine.

'I've been at sea,' said Ralph, who had spent his working life in a local factory, along with Brendan and the others, and had done nothing very exciting since retiring. He could imagine a life spent at sea. 'I never married.' That much was true. It's something he might have done differently – married, had children – if he had his time again.

A man about the same age as Elaine joined them, and Elaine introduced her brother Herbie and 'Mum's friend Ralph' to one another. A little girl who had tagged along, and who seemed to be Herbie's daughter, said to Ralph, 'I've got a goldfish.'

'A goldfish, eh?' said Ralph. 'I had a goldfish.'

'They only have three-second memories,' said the girl.

'Not so,' said Ralph. He had known that same fact as a boy. All his life, goldfish had been known to have three-second memories. Now, according to the newspapers, goldfish could remember things for weeks or even months. His goldfish, it turned out, had had an unsuspected wealth of memories. Instead of only ever knowing the most recent circuit of its bowl, it had perhaps, whilst living on Ralph's chest of drawers, still remembered the excitement of the fairground, the hook-a-duck stall at which it had been won, and perhaps, come autumn, it had still remembered the moments it had spent in a bucket in the garden on warm Sundays while Ralph cleaned its tank on the patio. That was a nice thought.

He told all this to the girl, who looked pleased and said, 'Then my goldfish probably remembers my birthday party.'

Elaine said to Ralph, 'You must come for something to eat.'

'Oh, I don't know,' said Ralph. It was not that he didn't want to – he was in no rush to get back to his empty flat or to go and sit at the corner table in his local all by himself. He very much wanted to accept Elaine's offer, but having told fibs about knowing Kathleen he was not sure that he could.

'I can show you my goldfish,' said the girl.

'Come on,' said Elaine, taking him by the arm.

The house was warm. Ralph made to take his shoes off at the door, so as not to spoil the nice carpet, but Elaine said, 'Don't worry about your shoes. Come in, come in.'

Herbie took Ralph's coat and hat and hung them on a peg in the hallway, then showed Ralph into the living room.

Offering Ralph a seat on the sofa, Herbie said, 'Make yourself comfortable.' A real fire was burning in the fireplace, in front of which was one of those armchairs that reclined. Ralph thought he'd rather like to try it out, although this didn't seem like the right moment.

'Sandwich?' asked Elaine, approaching with a laden plate. 'Sausage roll?'

'Can I get you a cup of tea?' asked Herbie. 'Or a cold beer?'

'Come and look at my goldfish!' said the girl, climbing up onto the sofa next to Ralph.

'Later, Sarah,' said Herbie. 'Let Ralph eat first.'

At some point, of course, Ralph would have to say that he hadn't really been Kathleen's sweetheart, that he hadn't actually known her at all. How nice it would be, though, to feel like one of the family – and it was such a lovely family – just for a little while, at least for as long as it took him to eat his sandwiches, his sausage roll, telling himself, *I will tell them soon*, as he accepted a cold beer from Herbie; thinking, *I should say it now*, while Elaine told a lively anecdote about Kathleen and then turned to Ralph to say, 'Isn't that just typical of Kathleen?' He had to say to them, 'The thing is . . .', and he would, of course he would, when the time was right.

Broad Moor

THE DIRT ROAD on the left went to Mere via Broad. Drew glanced at the directions that she had printed from the spa's website. *Take the second turn-off to Mere*, said the printout. *Do not take the first turn-off to Mere via Broad.* She was only a few miles from Mere now; she could be at the spa in time for a shower before the evening meal. She was going to need petrol though. She reckoned she could get there; it was the return journey she was really worried about. She was already into the red.

She pulled onto the verge and reached for her phone, to search online for a nearby petrol station, but she could not connect. She was about to drive on when she noticed a woman standing at the side of the dirt road. Drew wound down the passenger window and called out to her. 'Am I anywhere near a petrol station?'

The woman nodded. 'Take this left,' she said, indicating the turn-off. 'There's a petrol station in between Broad and Mere.'

Drew thanked her, pulled back onto the road and took the left turn towards Broad. Moorland reached in every direction, as far as the eye could see. It encroached on the dirt road, which looked as if it might peter out at any moment. She was relieved when she joined a proper road, single track but tarmacked, not a road you could get lost on.

It was supposed to be nice, the spa. Drew's friends, trying to persuade her that she needed a break, had said that the spa would be just the thing. Normally, after work, she went to the hospital, but today, when she left the office, she had set off for the spa at Mere, with her weekend bag already packed and stashed in the boot of her car. She and her friends would get massages and pedicures; they would use the hot tub and the sauna; they would sleep well and return home revived.

After months of cold weather, today had been bright and mild. It was getting chillier now, as the sun sank towards the horizon, but Drew kept her window down, letting in the fresh air and the smell of the moorland. There was a play on the radio, to which she was only half-listening.

At the top of an incline, Drew got her first glimpse of the sea: a flat line of blue-grey in the distance, which, as she drove on, slipped out of view before reappearing, closer than before. After a few miles, the moorland fell away to the right and Drew was driving alongside the North Sea. She had not noticed the radio play ending but now she was listening to music, to a song that was very familiar but which she could not place.

Drew would like to be here – at the coast, at the spa – with her sister. Kerry had been in a coma for more than three months now. She had lost a whole season, sleeping through the winter and into the first days of spring. It was tempting to think that the warmer weather might help, as if Kerry were like the eggs that they had incubated at primary school, most of which, kept warm beneath a bare light bulb, had hatched.

Drew had been resisting this weekend away, putting it off, because who else did her sister have? Their mother had dementia and no longer recognised them. Charlotte, who had been Kerry's girlfriend for almost a year, would not be visiting the hospital; she would not be allowed in if she tried. Not one of Kerry's Facebook friends had been to see her, despite saying they would. A few relatives had dropped by, but only Drew would visit Kerry every day. Only Drew brought in music to play for her sister, songs that Kerry might never have thought to say were her favourites but which were deep-down special, from the musicals they had loved growing up: 'Somewhere' from *West Side Story*, 'Over the Rainbow' from *The Wizard of Oz*. They were twins; they had a bond. Drew believed that playing these songs to Kerry, and talking to her for hours about everything and nothing, would give Kerry a sense of direction; the sound of the music, the sound of her voice, would enable her sister to move towards her, out of her coma and back into the real world. When Drew had said so, with conviction, a friend said, 'I suppose we can't really know what it's like for Kerry.' This troubled Drew, who did not really know what her sister had been through, what she was going through now, but who wanted to know.

The radio had gone to static. Drew pressed the button, finding station after station that was nothing but static. She was driving with her eyes on the radio when the shock of something hitting the windscreen made her slam on the brakes and she skidded a little before coming to a stop with her heart hammering. She got out of the car. In between the tyre marks that she had left on the road lay a garden bird. Drew approached. She crouched down and touched it, expecting it to flutter to life, but it continued to lie there, limp and unmoving. She hated to think that there might be a clutch of eggs in a nest somewhere, left to go cold.

Using a tissue, she moved the bird onto the verge, then got back behind the wheel and drove carefully away.

She could see no sign of civilisation, just the miles of moorland to her left and the cliff edge to her right.

She heard the six o'clock pips and the news headlines. She ought to phone her mother, who she spoke to each day at this time and who depended on her routines. Broad appeared to be a signal blackspot, but now she could see a red phone box such as she had not used since she was a child. These red phone boxes were an endangered species – abandoned, vandalised, decommissioned. She hoped that this one was still in working order. Just before it, there was a lay-by, in which she parked. When she turned off the engine, she could hear seagulls.

She checked her purse: she had plenty of coins. She got out of the car and walked to the phone box. A few feet to the right, the churning sea smashed against the cliff walls.

She had forgotten how heavy these phone box doors were; it took some effort to heave it open. She lifted the receiver off its hook and heard the reassuring dialling tone. She inserted her coins, dialled the number and waited until her call was answered.

Hello?

'Hello, Mum,' she said. There was a pause and then, again, that small voice at the end of the line.

Hello?

'Mum, it's Drew. Can you hear me?' She was in the middle of explaining where she was, when she realised that there was no one on the other end now; she could just hear the disconnect tone. She replaced the receiver and stood for a moment watching the seagulls wheeling over the moor, over the roof of a brown house at the end of a dirt track opposite the phone box.

Her eye was caught by a movement down the road, in the direction from which she had come, and she turned to see an approaching moped. As it neared, Drew recognised the stout figure of the woman to whom she had spoken at the junction.

Drew came to the edge of the road and flagged her down. When the woman had stopped and removed her helmet, Drew said, 'Is it far to the petrol station?'

'You're still in Broad,' said the woman, gesturing to suggest that Broad was the brown house, the dirt track, the red phone box, and the bare moorland all around. 'You won't see the petrol station till you're almost in Mere.' She eyed Drew. 'You look like you could do with a cup of tea. Come inside and I'll put the kettle on.'

'I'm afraid I can't stop,' said Drew. 'I have to meet friends. How far is it to Mere?'

'Not far,' said the woman. 'Not as far as it seems. Follow the road.'

Drew returned to her car. It would be just her luck, she thought, to find that the engine would not start, but it did. She drove on, watching her rear-view mirror, seeing the woman staring after her, until the cliff edge forced the road around a series of bends and the woman disappeared from sight.

She ought, while she was at the phone box, to have called her friends or the spa, to let them know that she was not very far away. If she was not there in time for the evening meal, she hoped that they would keep something warm for her.

After hugging the coastline for some miles, the road veered inland, across the moor. A dirt road went off to the side but, seeing no signpost to Mere, she kept to the road she was on. Since leaving the main road, she had seen no signposts at all. There was a map in the printed directions, but it did not show Broad; she could not see where she was. Coasting along with one hand on the wheel, she tried to connect to Google Maps, but there was still no signal.

She was receiving static again but, as the road returned to the edge of the moorland and Drew negotiated a stretch that came perilously close to the cliff edge, the radio fastened onto a foreign-language station. She was glad of it, the incomprehensible chatter, and what sounded like a cover of 'Copacabana'. She tried to sing along, but could not remember the words.

When the road turned inland again, she lost the foreign-language station. She fiddled with the tuner, but mainly there was only static, punctuated here and there by snatches of talk and old songs. Another dirt road went off to the side, but again there was no signpost. She had to trust the road: she had a poor sense of direction; she had got lost walking on moors before, and on Kinder Scout had gone so far wrong that she'd had to be helped by a stranger.

Coming to the top of an incline, Drew saw the sea again. The road found its way back to the cliff edge, which was no doubt eroding: in places, there was hardly any verge.

She noticed tyre marks on the tarmac and wondered if anyone ever went over the edge.

It was no wonder the directions warned against taking this particular route; the way the road snaked about might be adding hours to her journey.

It was amazing, she thought, just how long you could carry on running on fumes. Even after another few miles, it was not an empty petrol tank that brought her to a stop but the sight of another phone box. She pulled into a lay-by.

Drew heaved open the phone box door. She lifted the receiver and put it to her ear, listening for the dialling tone. She could hear only silence, as if the line had been disconnected. She supposed that out here in the middle of nowhere, these phone boxes were rarely used. She put the receiver back into its cradle and pushed open the door.

'You're lost.'

There was the woman, sitting astride her moped, and, behind her, at the far end of a dirt track, a lonely brown house. Drew looked at the phone box, and at the lay-by in which she was parked, and at the cliff edge beneath which the sea dashed itself against the rock. She sighed. 'I don't suppose I could use your phone?' she said. She was keen to call her friends or the spa, to say that she was close but that she had got lost, that she was in Broad, driving in circles. If they knew where she was, then if she failed to arrive – if she ran dry, broke down, in the middle of nowhere – help could be sent.

'Do you want that cup of tea now?' said the woman.

Drew, who really only wanted to leave, said, 'That would be lovely, thank you.'

'You'll have to leave your car here,' said the woman. 'The

track to the house is too narrow. The moped can do it.' She patted the seat behind her. 'Hop on.'

Drew climbed onto the back of the moped and rode – helmetless, pressed close to this stranger, whose bulky cross-body bag dug uncomfortably into Drew's leg – up the mile of narrow track to the brown house. She could not imagine living so far from civilisation; she would not be able to bear it. But this woman seemed tough, capable. The woman cut the moped's engine. 'In you come,' she said, ushering Drew inside before shutting the door.

Drew found herself standing in a large kitchen. It smelt of the moor, of the heather tied to nails in the ceiling beams. The woman took off her bag and set it down on the kitchen table, then turned to put the kettle on to boil. She fetched mugs and teabags out of a cupboard and lifted a biscuit tin down from a shelf.

'Would it be possible,' said Drew, 'for me to use your phone?'

'There's no phone,' said the woman, emptying the kettle into the two mugs, 'but there's a bed here for you.'

'Oh, no,' said Drew.

'It's all right,' said the woman. 'I'm on my own here with a spare room. The bed's already made up, with a clean sheet on the mattress. You can't reach Mere before dark now, whichever way you go. You'll have to stay here.'

'That's very kind of you,' said Drew, 'but I'm afraid I can't stay.'

'Here's your tea anyway,' said the woman, passing a mug across the table. 'Sit down.'

Drew sat, putting down her car keys and reaching for her tea.

'Where would you be without me?' said the woman, opening the biscuit tin and pushing it towards Drew.

Drew glanced at the clock on the wall. She ought to be at the hospital now. This was her visiting time.

Drew had not known much about Charlotte before Kerry began dating her. She had known that Charlotte was a lot older, and liked a laugh, and had a temper. Drew and Kerry had been sharing a flat, but when Drew left to go travelling, her sister had moved into Charlotte's house. Drew kept in touch with her sister through Facebook. Every few months, Kerry asked Drew when she was coming back. After nearly a year, in an exchange of comments beneath a picture of a shrine at sunset, Kerry said to Drew that she was going to move out of Charlotte's house. Within the hour, there was a comment from Charlotte: *You can't leave!*

Drew sipped at her hot tea. 'It's very kind of you,' she said again, 'but I really can't stay. I can drive in the dark.'

'Not on the moor,' said the woman. 'It's not safe.'

Drew pictured herself on the moor with night falling. She would drive into a bog and get stuck, or she would drive off a cliff. She would run out of fuel and be stranded in darkness, or she would drive in a circle again and end up back here.

She nodded. 'You're right,' she said. 'I'll wait here until it gets light again. Thank you.'

'Good girl,' said the woman.

'I should get my weekend bag from the car,' said Drew.

'The light will go before you can get there and back,' said the woman. 'I can give you a toothbrush.'

'Thank you,' said Drew. She could manage for one night, sleeping in her clothes, borrowing a few essentials.

Drew finished her tea and took a biscuit from the tin. Her friends would worry about her. First thing in the morning, she would get out of Broad, get off this moorland, but it would be crazy to attempt the journey now. She had found the landscape confusing enough in daylight.

What she really wanted was to go home. She was longing to see Kerry, whom she should never have left. It had taken her days to see that last Facebook message from her sister, and by the time Drew got back from Thailand, Kerry was in the hospital with rope burns on her wrists. Drew would never forgive herself.

As the woman locked the front door and moved to the window to draw the curtains, Drew looked and saw that the light was already going. It would be difficult even to follow that mile of dirt track across the moor in the gloom. And it would be suicidal to try to negotiate that unlit and eroding coastal road. She could not imagine, she thought – as she watched the woman unpacking her cross-body bag onto the table, wire cutters thumping down next to the biscuit tin – how desperate she would have to be to do that.

Pieces

LAST WEEK, IN Old Market Square, the boy ran through the jets of water in his Spiderman wellies, while his dad stood nearby saying *Be careful*, *Don't slip*, and his mum sat on a bench and watched, and then she shared a bar of chocolate between the three of them.

Today, the water is off. The boy does not know why. He keeps asking. The dry holes are not round like the fork marks in the pies that his mum used to make; they are oblong, the size of a grave they dug in the garden for a bird that had died.

His dad shares a chocolate bar between them and the boy cries because he does not want half; he only wants a third.

The Spite House

WHEN CONNOR DIED at the age of thirteen, his sister got his bike. It was a racer and better than her old one. Claire wrote in her diary that she preferred being an only child.

She left the bike and everything else behind when she went to Australia, living there for years until her fiancé broke off the engagement and her widowed father died, leaving her the family home.

She parks her hire car where her parents used to park the family car, the Austin Allegro with its square steering wheel. She feels as if she is intruding.

The house has a date chiselled into the stone above the front door. When Claire was little, she always wanted to know what it said. Her mother told her, '1741,' but her father would squint up at the stonework and tell her something different every time.

The house is not far from the river that runs through the village. Her mother had become obsessed with the possibility that the river might flood. The emails she sent to Claire in Australia mentioned sandbags. *But we don't know how many to get*, she wrote. *How many will be enough?*

There is a spit of rain in the air, and a chill. During her first year in Australia, it seemed strange to spend Christmas Day on the beach, in a bikini, barbecuing the Christmas dinner. Now, with summer left behind on the far side of the world, it is the prospect of a cold Christmas Day that will take some getting used to.

She gets out of the car with her suitcase and leftover food from the funeral that her aunt arranged and at which Claire was like a distant relative, a stranger. She had to keep explaining about her fiancé, and overheard someone using the word 'abandoned', which made her sound like a building, heading for dereliction.

The bony hedge pokes at Claire as she walks to the front door. She eyes the numbers chiselled into the stone as she passes beneath them, as if not entirely trusting that they will not change.

The hallway is cold. Even in the kitchen, the heart of the home, she can see her breath. She puts the clingfilm-covered food down near the sink. It is the middle of December but the heating has not been on for a while. The kitchen radio is on, though. She does not like to think of it having been on with no one to hear it, murmuring away in an empty house. It is tuned to a foreign station. She twists the dial but keeps coming back to this same station, this foreign language – French? She studied French at school, has been to France on holiday many times and can ask for what she wants in French shops and cafés, but standing in her parents' house, listening to what her guts tell her is French, she finds that she cannot understand a word that is being said.

She and her brother used to take turns sitting in the

front seat of the Austin Allegro. Connor always wanted the radio on; they had hours and hours of Radio Nostalgie during drives through France. In amongst the unfamiliar French songs were some in English – classics to which Connor knew all the words. Claire remembers him filling his lungs and blasting out 'My Way' and her being unable to get him to shut up, however much she yelled and screamed at him, their parents shouting, '*Both of you*, just stop it!' When Claire was in the front, she turned the radio off and played her cassettes, and Connor complained but there was nothing he could do while it was her turn.

It is surprising that the radio in the kitchen is able to pick up a French station, and that it is unable to pick up anything else.

She puts the kettle on but then finds that the only coffee in the cupboard is decaffeinated and has gone solid in the jar; and there is no milk – everything in the fridge is out of date. She cannot drink black coffee; she needs it milky and sweet. Apart from the funeral food, she has not brought any supplies with her. There are tins in the cupboard but when she tries to use the tin opener it comes apart in her hands, the tiny cogs falling to the floor and getting lost between and behind the units. Standing there in the middle of the kitchen holding on to that unbreached tin, she feels like the blind woman in *The Day of the Triffids*, clutching a tin of beans that she cannot get into.

Claire turns the radio off and looks out of the window. There used to be a scarecrow in the strawberry patch. Despite being little more than two big sticks lashed together, like a crucifix for warding off vampires or keeping demons at bay, the scarecrow was effective. It is no longer there though. There are birds on the fence. The swallows and wheatears and chiffchaffs that ought to be long gone by now are still hanging around, in the middle of winter. It isn't right.

'I think,' she says to herself, 'I shall go for a shower.'

Upstairs, in the bathroom, she locks the door even though she is alone in the house. She stands under the drizzling water, which is cold even though the knob is turned to hot. There is shampoo – for dry, damaged hair – but no conditioner, and she hasn't thought to bring her own. Her hair will be hard to untangle; it will dry in knots.

Claire has not worn pyjamas since she was a child, even in winter, but she is finding the house so cold that she regrets not having some with her. She has not been able to get the heating to come on, and has no idea why. She will have to call someone. She digs out one of her mother's old-fashioned nighties and puts that on. Its thin, off-white cotton reaches down to her ankles.

The sheets on her bed are probably clean but she hasn't slept there in so long that she changes them anyway. Her bedroom is long and narrow, like a corridor, no wider than the span of her arms, and next to it is Connor's which is just the same. They are two halves of what was once one big room, divided down the middle so that Claire and Connor would not have to share. Claire once read an article about spite houses – skinny, ugly constructions built by people holding grudges, people wanting to spoil the view or block the light or otherwise ruin the life of a hated neighbour, often a sibling. Some of them are hundreds of years old and still standing. These narrow and poorly lit rooms are just like that. In hers, now, she feels like Alice grown large in Wonderland where nothing is quite right.

She tries the door to Connor's room but finds it locked or stuck. She goes back to her own room and gets into bed. On the nightstand, there is a book that she must have been reading when she was last home. She picks it up, puts on her glasses and reads an Edgar Allan Poe story about a dead man whose heart seems still to beat beneath the floorboards. When she turns off the lamp, she remembers how she used to hate this long, dark room at night. She used to call her mother to put the hallway light on. Her bedroom door is ajar but the hallway light is off. Her funeral outfit, hanging on the back of the door, looks like someone standing in the shadows – it looks like herself standing there.

She can't get to sleep. She supposes that she is out of sync, still on Australian time, although she has been awake all day – according to her body clock the funeral took place in the middle of the night – and she feels tired. When she was younger, she suffered from insomnia and volunteered as a subject in a sleep laboratory. She knows from this experience that she might swear she's been awake all night when in fact she's been asleep. Here, now, she cannot be certain because no one has been watching her sleep.

She becomes aware of the sound of a man talking downstairs. 'It's not Dad,' she says to herself. Then she catches the French and hears music and understands that it is just the radio, which she thought she had switched off but must not have done. She does not go downstairs; she pulls the covers up to her throat and lies there listening until the room grows light. When she gets up, she feels the way a lack of sleep always makes her feel – a bit thin and unreal.

Today, she will unpack and then she will begin to feel

at home; she will go shopping for fresh food and make a start on the work she has brought with her; and she will start to make the house ready for Christmas. She takes an outfit out of her suitcase and puts it on. Both the top and the trousers are the beige of the sandbags her parents acquired, hoping to hold back the flood. (*Where do we have to put them? What should we do about the cat flap?*) Her top has a hole in it. She thinks of wet sand seeping out.

She goes downstairs and into the kitchen, where there is still no milk. The kitchen smells wrong. It smells of the river, of water thick with weeds, water in which a sheep once drowned. She empties the bin and clears out the fridge, throwing away the small, uneaten portions, finding nothing that explains that mouldering smell. She checks the cupboards and the utility room which houses the washing machine, the ladder, some tools and her bike, the racer, which has grown rusty. She investigates the washing machine, expecting to find it full of dirty water, but that is not it. She moves the bike and some of the tools, looking for a leak, some rot, but she cannot for the life of her find the source of that smell, the smell of the outside being inside.

Walking into the living room, she finds that she has in her hand the lump hammer from the utility room. She places it on the coffee table and sits down at the piano, which she played as a child – not as well as Connor but she got more certificates in the end. For a long time, Connor was confined to his bed and, when Claire practised, there was always the worry that she would wake him and then there would be trouble. Now, she lifts her hands to the old ivories, spreads her fingers so that she is poised above a chord, and presses down, but the keys are dead, something inside stuck or broken.

The work she has brought with her is the manuscript of a novel that is pretty much finished, almost ready to be sent out to agents; it is just in need of a final read-through. It is bright outside but dim in the house so she switches on a lamp before sitting down and beginning to read. She has read her novel through on many occasions, making small changes here and there. She is surprised to find that now, perhaps aided by her change of environment, she is seeing all sorts of things that she has never noticed before. Her first page alone is one dreary line after another. With a red pen in her hand, she begins scoring through lines and paragraphs and sometimes whole pages. In the middle of the afternoon, she goes to look at the funeral food, before returning to her manuscript without having touched a thing. The man in her novel is bothering her. He reminds her of her fiancé, with whom she was going to have children but who, quite suddenly it seemed, had a change of heart. She works into the evening, yawning as the sky goes dark, making her notes in the margins – *cut all this*, *NO*, *doesn't work . . .* , *doesn't make sense*. She throws an entire chapter into the bin and stands up, stretching, pleased to have cut out so much rot. There is more, though, she is sure, which will have to be dealt with another day. Looking at her watch, she sees how late it is and heads to the stairs. On the landing, she realises she is carrying the lump hammer with her.

Despite being so tired, Claire does not sleep well that night, or perhaps she does and only dreams that she is lying awake listening to all the French she seems to have forgotten; lying awake feeling terribly cold; lying awake thinking about her fiancé, her ex, who lives where it is warm and where it is not the middle of the night; lying awake listening to what sounds like birds in the loft, scratching at the floor as if they are trying to burrow through. Just before dawn, she says to the ceiling, 'Don't you ever sleep?'

In the morning, Claire walks down to the local shop. But where it ought to be, she finds a housing estate. She is standing staring at the row of private front doors when it starts to rain. She isn't wearing a coat and returns home – eyeing the '1741' as she passes beneath it to enter the house – with her jumper heavy with rainwater, a damp smell rising from her as she stands in the hallway. She smells like the sheep field, as if a gate has been left open and a sheep has got out, got into the house.

Upstairs, Claire peels off her wet jumper. The rain has seeped through to the top she has on underneath, like damp through layers of wallpaper. Her bare forearms are stippled with goose pimples. Standing between the too-narrow walls of this house that feels all wrong, she has a vision, suddenly, of how it should be, of what she will do. Instead of these dark, partitioned rooms there will be light and space. She has seen it done on television, on the old episodes of *Homes Under the Hammer* that they show in Australia – an archway knocked through here, a dividing wall knocked down there. She will start now, to make the house ready for Christmas. The lump hammer is on her bedside table. She picks it up, swings it to feel its weight, and then aims it at the partition wall. She thinks of her ex and what he would say if he could see her now. He says things like *drongo*, *gone troppo*; he speaks a different language.

This wall dividing her space from Connor's is surprisingly insubstantial; in no time at all, it is nothing but broken plasterboard at her feet. The room is twice the size and full of light now. Connor's bed, standing in one corner, looks bigger than hers, or maybe not bigger but just somehow imposing, as if this room were really his.

But still, there could be more space, more light. She crosses to the far side of the room, where it adjoins the master bedroom, and swings the hammer.

By the time it has grown too dark to see, she is standing by her parents' bed, looking at the wall that separates the bedroom from the bathroom. She has always wanted an en suite. She knows that she should stop. She should eat – she is hungry and wonders if she ate anything the day before; she can't remember. She should sleep. But she can't stop until it is finished; she is a woman possessed.

When she finally rests and looks around, she is astonished by how much she has done. Where there was carpet, there is now rubble and debris, which she has to negotiate to get to the door.

Downstairs, she roots about in the understairs cupboard, looking for the Christmas decorations, finding them at the back, next to a boxed-up, hundred-piece train track that Connor would have liked and which was very likely purchased for him but given to her instead. She never played with it much.

She carries the decorations into the living room. She has not yet got a tree but she hangs some tinsel over the mirror and puts some fairy lights around the door. Her mother spent hours shut away in the kitchen every Christmas, cooking so much food it could never all be eaten. Claire has always liked the idea of an open-plan kitchen-living room.

The nights here are long but eventually, from the living room, Claire sees daylight seeping in through the kitchen window.

She puts down the hammer and picks up her manuscript. Leafing through it, she can see that it still needs work. She sits down and takes the lid off her scratchy red biro.

When she finally stops, she is surprised by the amount of red ink on the pages (*get rid of this character altogether*). Parallel lines slash through her paragraphs like bloody gashes, scoring through the paper itself, taking out three pages in one go.

I'm starving, she thinks. Her stomach aches for food. In the kitchen, the funeral sandwiches and funeral vol-au-vents are still out on the side, but the clingfilm has been breached by flying shards and the food is covered in plaster dust. She looks at it, at this much-wanted meal that she cannot eat. The radio is on. She turns it off.

It seems to her that she has been awake for days. She goes up to the bedroom. The way it looks reminds her of those houses you sometimes see mid-demolition, with walls missing, the wallpaper in one room clashing with the wallpaper in the next, Connor's 1980s decor jarring between the adjacent rooms' neutral shades, and there is the moss-green, weed-green bathroom showing through that gaping hole she has made. She catches sight of herself in the mirror and is alarmed. Thin, and as dusty as the funeral leftovers, she looks like an exhumed corpse. She runs a bath, but it is cold and leaves her colder than ever.

She gets into her bed but, despite her exhaustion, she cannot sleep. Her bedding is scratchy, and she is too hungry, and it is too light. In the end, she climbs wearily out of bed and goes downstairs again.

On the table, there is just the lone title page of her novel. She looks at it and scores a red line through it. In the hallway, she puts on her coat. She will drive to a big supermarket to stock up, and to a DIY superstore for lily-white paint.

She stands on the doorstep, blinking in the weak, winter sunlight. It is snowing. When she and Connor were little, he was always, *always* the first awake, the one to make footprints in fresh snow. In her teens, though, *she* was the one to make those marks, the one to leave *her* footprints. She walks to her hire car, and as she gets in she glances back at the house and sees that the snow is already settling where she has stepped.

The snowy streets along which she drives are deserted. She doesn't see another soul until she pulls up in front of the twenty-four-hour supermarket. An elderly woman is walking a dog across the empty car park. Claire looks at the lowered shutters and winds down her window, calling out, 'Is the supermarket shut?' The woman, concentrating on the slippery tarmac, doesn't hear her and Claire has to raise her voice.

The woman, startled, turns and stares at Claire. 'Of course,' she says. 'Everything's closed for Christmas.'

'But it's not Christmas today, is it?' asks Claire.

'Yes, dear,' says the woman, looking at Claire as if she is mad. 'It's Christmas Day.'

Claire shakes her head, at the woman, at the supermarket,

as if it is the world, rather than herself, that is wrong. She drives back home. It is Christmas and she has no turkey or potatoes to roast, no sprouts or plum pudding to steam. She will have to try again to get into the tins – the soup and the beans. She will have to drink her coffee black, decaffeinated.

She rounds the final bend and brings the car to a standstill in the middle of the road, gaping. Half the house has collapsed. What used to be the living room is just a pile of bricks, burying the tinsel and the fairy lights. She can see the purple of Connor's bedroom wall. Even as she watches, part of the roof comes down. The kitchen has somehow survived though. The radio is on – she can hear 'My Way' blasting out.

The Meantime

'It would never do for me to come to life again.'
—Joseph Conrad, *The Secret Sharer*

THE JAMESES TOOK early retirement and bought an old house in the Peak District. They stood outside, looking up at its big, grey frontage, trying to decide on a name.

'It should be a name that says something about it,' said Mrs James.

'Bleak House,' said Mr James.

They called it The Rambles. They were going to run it as a boarding house, providing bed and breakfast for the walkers who came to explore the Dark Peak.

Running a boarding house was something Mrs James had always wanted to do. She imagined herself receiving her guests in the dining room in the morning, offering them a choice of cereals and eggs, writing down their orders on a notepad. Her dolls, when she had played this as a child, had liked cornflakes and scrambled eggs.

Mrs James had grown up in a house that was old and grey just like The Rambles, although it had been smaller, much smaller, and was squeezed between others in a terrace, whereas this one was in the middle of nowhere. When Mrs James was quite young, her father had become unwell, in need of bed rest, and her mother had nursed him. Her mother would say, 'This afternoon, we might go to the park, but in the meantime your father's sleeping and you must be quiet, Jacqueline.' Her father's meals had to be taken to his bedroom on a tray, and sometimes this job was given to Jacqueline. She always hoped to find him sleeping, and went on tiptoe, trying not to let the cutlery rattle against the plate, so that she would not wake him up by going in.

The Rambles had six en-suite bedrooms including their own. Mr James, a numbers man, entertained himself by referring to the room numbers in binary, which made it sound as if they were running an enormous hotel with more than a hundred rooms spread over the three floors. As it happened, they could not even fill the five guest rooms they had; business was quiet. Mr James said that they should get a website, but for that they would need to be connected to the internet. Recently, wanting to send off for some diet pills that she had seen advertised in a magazine, Mrs James had needed to take two buses to use the internet in the nearest library. Her order was being sent from abroad, but in the meantime she had heard on the radio that these diet pills were highly toxic, containing, as they did, dinitrophenol, which was a pesticide, apparently. Even a couple of these tablets could prove lethal within hours. A few clicks of the mouse and she had, it turned out, ordered poison. She was quite sure that they would all be better off without the internet. Her father had disliked modern technology; he had never allowed the family to have a television set, which in any case would have been too noisy. Mrs James had instead spent much of her girlhood with her own thoughts, her imagination.

Mr James, who had worked in the city, was infuriated by the complete lack of mobile phone signal. 'It's like living in the Dark Ages,' he said, standing on the landings and in the garden, holding his phone up in the air, but Mrs James was quite satisfied with the landline, and the post box which was only a short walk away.

Perhaps, she thought, she could make the journey into town again and ask the doctor for a safer diet pill, but in the meantime she was simply depriving herself of all the things she loved, the comfort food that made her fat.

Room five, at the top of the house, was let to a writer who never came down to breakfast and instead drank coffee alone in his room, leaving his dirty cups outside his door for Mrs James to wash. She refused to take his breakfast up to his room, not that he asked. Perhaps he had food in there with him. There would be crumbs. Mrs James wanted to get in and clean but she had given each room a 'DO NOT DISTURB' sign and room five's seemed permanently to hang on the outside of his door. He never went out and she would not clean his room while he was in it. For a year or two in her teens, she had worked as a chambermaid in a hotel. She hadn't minded it – the vacuuming, the wiping things down, the straightening things up. Except once, a man had remained in his room while she cleaned it. He had been lying on the bed, on his back, with his shirt and trousers on, his tie and belt on the bedside table. Silently, he had watched her work and she had hated that. When she went to his bedside table to remove a dirty coffee cup, he turned towards her and she thought he was going to touch her, although he didn't. She had finished the room quickly and left without a word having been said.

The house could be quiet for days on end. When the phone rang, it was a shock, and Mrs James would hurry to answer it, not wanting room five to be disturbed. She knew that the writer himself was not expecting calls; he wanted no interruptions while he was finishing his book. There were silent retreats, she had said to him when he first arrived, where no one was allowed to have mobile phones or to speak at all. 'Sounds wonderful,' he had said, and, with a last, polite smile, closed his door.

A mother came with her little girl for a short stay, and Mrs James put them in room one, as far as possible from the writer. Even so, when the girl, who must have had a bad dream, began crying in the middle of the night, wailing like a baby, Mrs James lay in bed, tensed, thinking, 'Be quiet, be quiet, be quiet.' Tomorrow night, she thought, she would take a sleeping pill, and she could give one to the writer too.

The mother and the little girl did come down to breakfast. Mrs James met them in the dining room, showed them to their seats and said first to the mother and then to the little girl, 'Would you like your eggs poached, boiled, scrambled or fried?'

'No, thank you,' said the girl.

Mrs James looked at her with surprise. She gave the girl a patient smile and said, 'You have to choose one.'

'I don't want eggs,' said the girl.

Mrs James's face stiffened and she turned to the mother.

The mother said to the girl, 'You'll have some toast, though, won't you?'

'White or brown?' asked Mrs James, her new note pad and her silver pen held tightly at chest height, like a tiny sword and shield. She would not look at the girl now, and addressed her question to the mother. Even when the girl, with her little face turned towards Mrs James, said, 'White, please,' Mrs James did not look at her, but kept her eyes on the pad, on what she was writing, and then nodded at the mother and went back into the kitchen.

She could hear the girl talking to her mother in a high, loud voice. 'Did you know,' said the girl, 'ghosts are exactly the same colour as the air?'

'Ghosts aren't real,' said her mother, but the girl carried on as if her mother had not even spoken, talking on and on, and Mrs James waited for the mother to say, 'Shush, shush now.' Mrs James looked at the air, felt its stillness, its closeness, and then the toast popped up and made her heart race.

After breakfast, while the mother and the little girl were out, Mrs James cleaned their room, and then she stood outside room five, listening. She could not hear anything apart from the occasional creak. The 'DO NOT DISTURB' sign was hanging from the door handle. She went away again.

She and Mr James ate lunch together in the kitchen, and Mr James said, 'The chap in room 101—'

'Shhh,' said Mrs James, glancing up at the ceiling, even though room five was three floors away.

Mr James continued in a lower voice: 'How long is he staying?'

'I'm not sure,' said Mrs James.

'You'd better ask him.'

'Yes.'

At suppertime, Mrs James took the writer a boiled egg, meaning to knock on his door, offer him the egg, and ask him if he knew how long he would be with them, and if she might come in and clean his room. But in the end, she left the plate outside his door and did not knock.

She found the plate there in the morning, the debris spilling over its edge, onto the carpet, like a barrier of broken eggshell to keep the slugs away.

In the middle of the following night, the phone rang. Mrs James woke suddenly and reached for the handset, murmuring into the mouthpiece, into the darkness, 'Hello?' She handed the phone to Mr James. 'It's for you,' she said.

While Mr James spoke on the phone, Mrs James switched a lamp on and waited. When Mr James put the phone down, he said to Mrs James that his mother had had a fall, and that he would have to go and see her. 'She's been made comfortable for now.'

Mrs James thought of her father and his long illness. They had tried to make him comfortable. She had watched her mother crushing a sleeping tablet between the back of a spoon and the chopping board. 'He needs to sleep,' her mother had said. 'Tomorrow, I'll try to think of something nice we can do, but in the meantime your father's not well and we have to stay inside and be quiet.' Or her mother would say, as she slipped the powder into her father's warm milk, 'We might be able to go to the funfair at the weekend, but in the meantime you can play quietly at home.' Jacqueline, left to her own devices, had played with her dolls.

Mr James was dressing, buttoning his trousers, which he held up with braces, although he would rather have worn a belt.

'Are you going now?' whispered Mrs James.

'Yes,' he said. 'She's been asking for me. I might need to stay for a few days. Will you be all right?'

'Oh yes,' said Mrs James with a quick smile. 'Don't worry about me.'

Other than Mr James ringing regularly to check that she was all right, there were no phone calls, but a man came in person. Tall and broad, he filled the doorway. He announced that he needed a room for a week, and his voice filled the hallway.

'I suppose I could put you in . . .' began Mrs James.

'What's that?' said the man, turning his head so as to hear her better.

Mrs James made an effort to raise her voice and said, 'I could put you in a downstairs room.'

'Marvellous!' boomed the man. He clapped his hands together and the sound was like a gunshot.

She could hardly turn him away, when he needed a room and she had one free, and when business was still rather slow, but she was going to find it hard to bear, his big voice disturbing the household, carrying up and down the stairs and through the walls and floorboards. It made her terribly anxious, as if her father might yet appear on the landing, complaining about the racket, his belt in his hand, the tan leather gripped in his fist, the buckle shiny.

They were all in the living room, all of them except for the writer. The little girl was showing the loud man the words and actions to a song, which Mrs James recognised from her own childhood. Circling her hands around each other, the girl sang, at a moderate volume, 'Wind the bobbin up, wind the bobbin up, pull—' and here she changed the hand action, '—pull, clap, clap, clap.' The loud man was trying to follow, singing and winding and pulling and patting his hands together, both he and the girl giggling when he made a mistake. Then the girl sang it over again, but very quietly, almost whispering it. '*Wind the bobbin up, wind the bobbin up* . . .' The third time, she sang it quietly again but at breakneck speed: '*Windthebobbinup, Windthebobbinup* . . .' Mrs James laughed and everyone looked at her. Then the girl began to sing the verse once more, but now she sang it loudly, terribly loudly, yelling it out – 'WIND THE BOBBIN UP! WIND THE BOBBIN UP!' – and Mrs James said, 'Stop it! Please, stop it, you must stop,' and they all went quiet. Mrs James heard movement at the top of the house, and everyone watched her, and then there came the sound of a door closing and the house fell silent again. 'You can sing quietly,' said Mrs James, but the mother said perhaps they had sung enough, and her guests all said goodnight and went to their beds.

Mrs James remained in the living room for a little while longer, listening to the ticking of the clock, and then she went through to the kitchen to make some supper. She took a tin of soup out of the cupboard, and her pills. While she waited for the soup to heat through, she filled up her water glass, put out her sleeping tablet, and prepared a tray for room five. Very carefully, she carried the tray, the bowl of soup, up to the top of the house and set it down on the carpet outside the writer's room. The tray bumped slightly against the door, and the spoon rattled against the china bowl. Mrs James did not wait to see if the door opened. She went back down to the kitchen, ate her soup and took her sleeping tablet. Then she went around the house closing curtains and locking doors. The writer had taken in his supper tray. Mrs James listened at the door for a moment and then went to bed.

In her room, she said her prayers, put on her sleeping mask and slept until dawn. When she lifted up her mask, she saw the light seeping in around the blackout blinds. She felt quite refreshed.

She dressed, made herself presentable, and left the bedroom. Pausing once more outside room five, Mrs James, in spite of the 'DO NOT DISTURB' sign, gave a tentative knock. There was no reply. She would leave him for now, she thought. Later, she would unlock his door, check on him, take away his soup bowl, wash it up. She would dispose of the diet pills. She had only used a handful. What a waste, she thought. But it had to be done, and now she must open all the curtains, lay the table for breakfast, put out the cereals . . . She heard a downstairs toilet flushing, and someone laughing, the child waking up.

Common Ground

'I'm Gordon from next door,' he said, standing on Erica's doorstep, holding out a hand for her to shake. She had been expecting the postman, and for a moment she just looked at this man, at his neat silver hair and his well-trimmed moustache, his buttoned-up cardigan and his hand, which, when she took it, was cool and dry.

For a few months, that was how she would refer to him: 'Gordon from next door', or just 'Gordon'. Now she calls him 'Mr Granger' or 'that man'.

'I've just moved in,' he said. 'I thought I'd come and introduce myself.'

'I'm Erica,' she said. There was a pause, during which she thought she ought to say something like, 'You'll find us all very friendly round here,' but that was not quite true, or, 'Let me know if you need anything,' but she would rather he did not. The two of them listened to Erica's kettle coming to the boil.

'I haven't found my kettle yet,' said Gordon. 'It'll be in one of the boxes.'

Erica nodded.

'The problem is,' said Gordon, 'the boxes aren't labelled, and there are so many of them.'

'Ah,' said Erica.

'I've no milk anyway,' said Gordon.

She asked him in, and he thanked her and stepped into her hallway. She thought of vampires, who could not come in until they were invited. She closed the door behind him.

Gordon was looking at the piles of paperwork on the kitchen table.

'I'm in the middle of marking some work,' said Erica.

'I can see that,' said Gordon.

Erica got an extra mug out of the cupboard and set about making the coffee.

'I've seen you,' said Gordon, 'in your garden.'

He would be able to see her from his back door, or from his bedroom windows. Handing him his mug of coffee, she said, 'I've made it milky so it ought to be cool enough to drink straight away.'

He set the mug down on the table and took a seat. When he was settled, he said to her, 'Is there a Mr . . . ?'

'No,' said Erica. She sipped her coffee, which was too hot after all and burned her lip.

Gordon looked around, eyeing the framed photographs on the sideboard. There was no picture of her ex, not in her kitchen, not anywhere in the house. Her neighbour could go through this place with a fine-tooth comb and find precious little evidence that she'd ever had a husband. She had not said his name in years; she refused to talk about him, even to their daughter.

Gordon was looking through the window, admiring her tree. 'You have a cotoneaster,' he announced.

'Yes,' said Erica. 'Cotoneaster frigidus.'

'A member of the rose family,' said Gordon knowledgeably.

A rope ladder dangled from the lowest branch, like an invitation to climb. Erica had planted the tree herself, before Sophie was born. Later, Sophie had used the rope ladder to reach what she called her treehouse, though there was no house there, no structure, just the tree itself, within whose cradle of branches Sophie liked to sit. But she liked it too much; she spent hours in that imaginary treehouse, while Erica was alone in the house, washing up or hoovering or marking papers at the kitchen table. Erica would call to her, through the window, 'Are you going to come in now?' and Sophie would call back, 'No, not yet, I like it out here.' What if someone abducted her? One day, Erica would look out and find her gone, the branches empty. She liked to have her daughter safe inside the house, but Sophie was too independent.

Erica had imagined losing her daughter in so many different ways. In the toddler years, she feared her climbing a bookcase or a chest of drawers that had not been fastened to the wall and would crush her. When she was older, but still so little really, the fear was that she would go beyond the end of the garden, which was not allowed, and drown in the river. When Sophie was in her teens, Erica worried about her getting into cars with boys who would try to impress her with terrible speeds on the winding roads.

'You have a child,' said Gordon, 'or children?'

'No,' said Erica, eyeing the rope ladder. 'That needs to come down.'

Gordon moved to the window, watching the fieldfare that had come to eat the cotoneaster's berries. He said, through the double glazing, to the oblivious bird, 'You're a beauty, aren't you?' Gordon would have stayed there all morning, drinking Erica's coffee and admiring the birds, if she had let him.

He popped round for milk and sugar and onions, and sometimes she let him come in. They drank coffee and watched for fieldfares.

He asked her if she would like to swap keys.

'What for?' said Erica.

'You know,' said Gordon. 'If you go on holiday and want me to feed your cat, that sort of thing.'

'I'm not going on holiday,' said Erica. 'And I don't have a cat.'

'But you know what I mean,' said Gordon. 'If you're not here when a package arrives, or if you lock yourself out.'

'I don't intend to lock myself out,' said Erica.

He came round for jump leads, which she did not have, and asked her to go for a drink.

'A drink?' said Erica.

'A drink,' said Gordon. 'A glass of wine, or whatever you want.'

'No,' said Erica. 'Thank you.'

Gordon bowed his head on her doorstep before walking away.

The next time he asked, she told him, 'No, please don't ask me again.'

'It's only a bloody drink,' said Gordon.

Each time he asked, he was angrier. She stopped asking him in for coffee. If he wanted an onion, she gave it to him on the doorstep. He told her that they had a lot in common. She did not think so at the time. He liked military history, which left her cold. He chain-smoked on his back doorstep every morning and every evening, and she could not stand the smell.

Now she sees what they have in common.

The next time he knocked, it was to tell her that her tree dropped its leaves into his garden, spoiling his lawn. He'd had enough of it, he said, and he was going to cut her tree down.

'The tree is on my property,' said Erica. 'Cutting it down would be trespass.' She knew her rights.

She saw him later, out in the sun without his sunhat, red in the face, up a ladder with a hacksaw, cutting off the branches that hung over his wall.

But her leaves still blew his way and he could not stand it. 'And the roots,' he said, on her doorstep, 'go under my lawn. The roots are on my property, and I don't want them there.' He told her he was looking into chainsaws.

She stopped answering the door to him, but when she marked her students' work at the kitchen table, the cotoneaster with its missing branches was always at the edge of her vision.

Now she sits with her back to the window. She pulls another piece of work from the pile and looks at the opening paragraph. She shakes her head. Her red pen scrapes through the page. The students complain about her. They say she is too harsh, too set in her ways, and getting worse. But *this* and *this* and *this* – she purses her lips and prunes their work with blows of her red pen – is simply unacceptable and she will not allow it in her class. She has to tell them over and over again, and still they keep on making the same mistakes. She sees the looks on their faces when she hands back their brutalised work. She knows how they talk about her. They say things like, 'She's got it in for me.' But she does it because she cares, she really does care, about them and what they could achieve, under her guidance. She wants them to understand what she expects of them, and for them to be better, to deliver, or there will be more red marks; there will be a gradual lowering of grades; there will be penalties.

'We're moving to New Zealand,' said Sophie. 'We' was Sophie and her boyfriend, one of those boys who had come, after all, in his fast car to take her away. She said it cheerfully, as if it were a wonderful thing to be going so far away from her mother, thousands and thousands of miles away from her mother, who had never lived anywhere but here in this town.

'For how long?' asked Erica.

'Well,' said Sophie, and she did at least have the decency, then, to look ashamed, 'indefinitely.'

'But what about your job?' said Erica. It was a better job than anything Erica had had at that age, but Sophie just shrugged and said there were jobs in New Zealand.

'You'll regret it,' said Erica.

That's what her own mother had said when Erica had a foot of healthy hair cut off: 'How could you cut off your beautiful hair? You'll regret it.' And Erica *had* regretted it, but she did not let her mother see that. She kept her hair short out of stubbornness; she has kept it short to this day.

Erica tried, when talking to her daughter about this ridiculous plan, to stay calm, not to shout, but it had become more and more difficult. When the day of departure finally arrived, Erica refused to drive Sophie and the boyfriend to the airport. While Sophie was at the terminal, Erica was furiously stripping her daughter's bed. While Sophie was up in the air, Erica was emptying her daughter's room. She put the furniture into a skip. If Sophie tried to come back, she would find her bed gone, along with all those little keepsakes and cuddly toys she had left behind. It was heartbreaking to pull down her daughter's posters and hand-drawn pictures, to steam off the childish wallpaper. Erica painted the walls with what she had in the shed – something neutral, muted – and moved in a sofa bed that no one had ever used.

Erica will not pick up Sophie's phonecalls or open her letters, which come less frequently now. Sophie will be busy. She was pregnant when she left, so by now there will be a baby, presumably. The last time Erica went to the pharmacy, she found herself looking at the baby things while she was in the queue, looking at bibs and spoons and nappies. The pharmacist had to raise his voice to get her attention. 'Just my prescription,' she told him, moving forward.

By the time she got back, it was done. The branches of her cotoneaster were lying like a tangle of limbs in her garden, next to the severed trunk, the rope ladder drooping over them. So that was that. She would not speak to him about it; she would not give him the satisfaction.

The stump was still alive; it would need treating or it would rot, become diseased.

She can imagine how he is feeling now: righteous and miserable. There is no going back. When he stands on his doorstep with his cigarettes, what he will see is his ugly stump, the fieldfares gone.

The roots are still there, of course, snaking under his immaculate lawn, reaching in every direction. He will have trouble getting them out.

Burning the Winter

At half past four, the sun went down, and soon after that it was dark. The men lit the vast bonfire with burning, rag-wrapped sticks, like the torches that mobs carried hundreds of years ago. The bonfire had been standing ready, huge and dry, for days, and it was amazing, really, thought Katie, that no one had been tempted to burn it down before tonight.

The smoke from the bonfire was blowing her way and making her eyes sting, and with it came smouldering flakes of ash that Katie hoped would not burn holes in her brand new coat. The flames were creeping up towards the Guy, and Katie felt rather sorry for him, with his newspaper-stuffed limbs and his drawn-on face, smiling as if he were sitting on a throne instead of a pyre.

The volunteers in the scout hut were selling hot food. Katie and David went inside and bought two pots of mushy peas, which David carried back to the bonfire. Katie, mindful of the hot pots in his bare hands said, 'Are you all right with those?' and David said he was but a moment later, he said, 'I can't do this.'

'Let me take them,' said Katie, pulling her sleeves down

to cover her hands, to protect them from the heat coming through the polystyrene cups.

'No,' said David, 'I mean *this*,' and he tried to gesture, to express something more than just the peas that he was holding, but his meaning was still not clear to Katie. 'I mean *us*,' he said.

'Oh,' said Katie.

The Guy on top of the bonfire was alight now, and whoever was in charge of the fireworks, out there in the dark on the far side of the playing field, lit the first rocket.

'Do you still want your peas?' asked David.

'But what about the flat?' said Katie, later. She and David had taken out a joint mortgage. They had held hands as they sat in the mortgage adviser's office, except for when they had to let go to sign on the dotted line. And they had just that month bought a new bed, and new bedding, and towels.

'You should keep the flat,' said David. 'I'll move out.'

'What about the kitten?' said Katie. The kitten was five months old and liked to sleep at David's feet, although Katie was the one who put food in his bowl and cleaned his litter tray. They'd had a cat flap put into the back door, so that when the kitten was older he would be able to come and go, although before they could let him roam free he had to have what Katie called 'his little operation' and what David called 'his nuts cut off'.

'You can keep the kitten,' said David.

'What about Bognor Regis?' said Katie. They were due to go away to the seaside for a week in February, during the half-term holiday. They had already booked the hotel and the coach. The costs were non-refundable.

They had to stick to school holidays because of Katie's job in the school office, not because they had children; they did not have children, although they had talked about it – 'I don't want to leave it too late,' she had said.

'You can still go to Bognor Regis,' said David.

'What about the cool box?' said Katie, on the phone. She had pulled the cool box out of the understairs cupboard when she was looking for her suitcase. The cool box had come with them on all their summer holidays. Driving through the Alps, they had stopped to put snow in the cool box so they could have ice-cold drinks later. After driving all the way to the Mediterranean coast, they had opened up the cool box again and found that it was still full of this incongruous snow.

The cool box had belonged to David's parents, for whom it had been a honeymoon present, but they were dead now.

'You can keep the cool box,' he said.

On the coach to Bognor Regis at the start of her week off, Katie sat next to a woman who might have been eighty years old. The woman was reading a large-print book and caught Katie glancing at it. 'Flash fiction,' said the woman. 'I'm not sure I like it. You're waiting for it to really get going and all of a sudden, there's the ending. You've hardly started and it's all over.' She turned a page. 'Some of it's quite good though,' she added. She held out a hand. 'I'm Adele,' she said. She had an accent that Katie liked.

'Katie,' said Katie, shaking Adele's hand. 'I wasn't

supposed to be coming on holiday on my own,' she said, and she explained about David.

'More fool him,' said Adele.

'He told me on Bonfire Night,' said Katie, and she told Adele about the hot pots of peas that neither of them could eat, and the Guy with his drawn-on smile burning to nothing in moments, and everyone cheering as the fireworks went up.

'Where I come from,' said Adele, 'Bonfire Night is in February. We don't have Guy Fawkes Night of course. When we light our bonfires, we are burning the winter.'

'I like the sound of that,' said Katie, looking through the huge windows at the still-bare branches of the trees. They got onto the motorway and Adele turned back to her book briefly before saying to Katie, 'Sixty-six words! This story is sixty-six words long!' She shook her head in disbelief, but read on, smiling from time to time.

Katie was sitting alone at a table in the hotel's breakfast room when Adele appeared at her shoulder, saying, 'This is my all-time favourite song.'

Katie had not been paying attention to the background music, but she listened now. It was an old one: 'You've Lost That Lovin' Feelin'' by The Righteous Brothers.

'May I join you?' asked Adele, sitting down at Katie's table with a yoghurt and a spoon. 'When this single was released,' she said, peeling back the lid of her yoghurt, 'the radio stations would not play anything that was longer than three minutes and fifteen seconds. This song had a running time of three minutes and five seconds printed on the label, so the radio stations would play it, even though the running time was actually three minutes and forty-five seconds, far too long.' They listened to the remainder of the track while they ate, and when it finished Adele said, 'It's still very short though.'

'Do you have any plans for the day?' asked Katie, and Adele said she did not.

'Would you like to walk down to the beach with me?' asked Katie.

'That would be nice,' said Adele, and she scraped the last of her yoghurt off the silver foil lid and went back to the buffet for another pot.

It was a cold day but it was bright. Katie walked Adele down to the promenade, where they sat on a bench and drank polystyrene cups of hot tea, and Katie wondered whether the kitten, who had now had his little operation, was missing her.

Adele reached into her pocket and took out a leaflet, the hotel's programme of evening entertainment. 'Are you planning on going to the entertainment lounge tonight?' asked Adele. Katie had been planning on skipping that part of the day. She had imagined early nights: a warm bath and a sleeping mask and anything else that would help her to sleep, but Adele seemed disappointed by this. So instead, after dinner, Katie went to Adele's room, where she found her waiting in a sequined dress, with a zip at the back that Adele needed help with: 'I can't reach back there these days,' she said. Katie zipped her up and admired the array of evening dresses in Adele's wardrobe. 'Well,' said Adele, as Katie ran her hand through the silks and the spangles before closing the wardrobe door, 'you only live once.' They went together to the entertainment lounge where they sat through a comedian who was not very good, although Adele's asides made Katie smile.

The following day, Katie looked up the opening times of a local museum and took Adele there on the bus. In the evening, she collected Adele from her room again and accompanied her to the entertainment lounge.

On the third morning, over breakfast, Adele looked at Katie with bright grey eyes and said, 'I've got a date! With a much younger man,' she added, winking. 'He's only seventy-three. He's taking me to the park this morning, and then to a matinee at the cinema, and tonight he wants to take me dancing.'

'Oh,' said Katie. 'That's great.'

After breakfast, Adele went up to her room to get herself ready for her day out, and Katie went down to the cold beach, where she went for a ride on the miniature train that ran on wheels along the promenade. She thought it would take her all the way along the seafront, but it did not even make it as far as the pier before turning around and coming back, and everybody got off.

Katie thought about staying in her room that evening, having that early night she'd had in mind. After a bath, she got as far as putting on her pyjama bottoms, but it was not even nine o'clock and she could hear the disco booming through the floor of her room, and in the end she got dressed and went along.

She got herself a drink from the bar and sat down at the only free table she could find. The dance floor was crowded and the people looked happy but Katie was thinking about David, and how cold it had been just beyond the reach of the bonfire, and how the fireworks had probably cost thousands of pounds and had gone up and gone out in a matter of minutes.

All the songs were old, and Katie was wondering if she had made a mistake in coming here. Perhaps she ought to go back to her room and have that early night, and then in the morning, she could leave. She took a sip of her drink, a beer with an unexpected aftertaste that she could not decide whether she liked: it was sharp and sweet, citrussy. It went down easily enough. She was putting down her empty glass and getting to her feet, just realising that she recognised the song that had come on, when a hand touched her shoulder. Katie looked up and saw Adele standing there in her brightest dress.

'There you are,' said Adele. 'Are you coming to dance with us? They're playing my all-time favourite song.' She took Katie's hand. 'Come on, it's already halfway through,' she said, and Katie let herself be led into the heat of the dance floor, into the throng of those who were already up and dancing to this short song.

Hardanger

SUE WAS IN-BETWEEN. No longer really a child but not quite an adult either. She was as tall as her mother but still slept with her teddy bear. She was still at school but on Fridays she went to the pub with her friends, where they drank squash and ate crisps. She had a Saturday job, and with her wages she bought jewellery made out of sweets. Her bedroom door had a sign on it saying, 'NO ENTRY ☠ KEEP OUT'.

In her bedroom, Sue had a collection of road signs that had been brought home under cover of darkness and sneaked inside while Marlene and Bill watched the news. Marlene saw them when she hoovered – she saw the red-rimmed triangles on rusting legs, the silhouetted workmen and exclamation marks. She stood in the doorway, pushing the vacuum cleaner into the room without stepping over the boundary herself. There were letters, too, the sort that belonged on shopfronts. Sue had the curving 'S' and the vowels of her Christian name. The metal prongs of the 'U' and the 'E' looked lethal. They made Marlene think of her great uncle who lost his eye to a garden fork, apparently. She has never been able to conceive quite *how*, quite how this could have happened, and so she keeps imagining it happening in all sorts of not-quite-right ways.

Marlene imagined the holes in the road that were now missing their attendant warnings, and the businesses in whose names gaps had appeared overnight. When she asked Sue to get rid of these things, Sue expressed indignation. 'My signs?' she said.

'But they're *not* yours,' said Marlene. 'They shouldn't be in the house.'

With a dismissive gesture, Sue agreed to get rid of them. 'I'll take care of it,' she said. But still they remained.

'I don't know what to do with them,' said Marlene to Bill, but he just shook his head and shrugged. It bothered Marlene endlessly that they were there, but she couldn't carry them – as heavy and awkward as they were – back into town. She didn't want to take them on the bus. Not knowing the best way to get rid of them, she left them where they were, in Sue's bedroom. She shut the door.

It was almost a year since Marlene and her girls had moved from the farm in the Midlands to that coastal town, to Bill's house. Marlene was still adjusting. She found it odd, to be so close to water, to the sea and the mouth of a river, and yet, out in the suburbs, to be steeped in concrete slabs and pebble dash. Her younger daughter had acclimatised quickly. Lizzy liked living near the seaside, and she liked Bill and called him 'Dad'. It had occurred to Marlene that Lizzy might be young enough not even to remember her real father in due course. Sue, on the other hand, was not even trying. She resented the move and her mother's remarriage. She did not call Bill 'Dad'. She missed the farm and her father, who used to take her out walking in the countryside, where she would fill her pockets with stones, and leaves that harboured insects, and pine cones that closed up when it was going to rain, as if they knew, like the cows lying down in the fields, like the birds flying low. She unloaded them in the kitchen, making her own nature table, and Marlene said that it was very nice, but must it come into the house?

There was a boy, a disarmingly beautiful boy who never quite made eye contact. He came to the house and hung around, or else he took Sue out. He was older than Sue, although still just a child himself really.

'Is she old enough,' said Marlene to Bill, 'for a boyfriend?'

'Do you want me to warn him off?' asked Bill.

'No,' said Marlene. 'Keep him close.'

When Sue said that she wouldn't go with them to Norway at Easter, they said she could invite the boy, Travis, to join them.

'Sure,' said Travis, when Sue asked him. 'Whatever.' He was sitting in Bill's armchair and spoke without looking up from the guitar at whose strings he was plucking.

'Good man,' said Bill, who was sitting in the cat's place on the sofa.

Marlene took Sue late-night shopping for new clothes, going by train into Plymouth. The light was going and it had started to rain. Looking out through the window, Marlene saw a field, grey beneath the stormy sky, a wide expanse of long, dense grass rippling in the wind. Then she saw that the whole field was shifting; it was rising and falling like something alive, and she realised that it wasn't a field at all, but water, the river Plym.

◊

In Oslo, they took photos of the docks, churches, the palace and the patrolling guards. Later, looking at the images on the screen of the camera, Marlene said, 'Did we not take any family photos? We should, just to prove we were here.'

They travelled west to the outskirts of Hardanger and unloaded the car, taking their luggage into their cabin, Travis carrying his guitar. He could not really play it but he wanted to learn, he said to Bill, because it was a good way to get girls.

In Hardanger, a district known for apple blossom and cider, fiddles and folklore, they posed in front of the mountains for photos of the family, which Travis took. The sunlight gave Sue, with her fine blond hair, a halo, as if she were a young girl saint. *Like Joan of Arc*, thought Marlene, and then, quickly, *No, not Joan of Arc*. 'Smile,' said Travis, and they all smiled.

But later, when they were back at the cabin and they looked at the photos, they found that Bill and Marlene had been chopped off; there were only the girls, standing alone with the sun in their eyes, and, behind them, the immense mountains, and the V of sky between them. 'I'm no good with technology either,' said Marlene to Bill. 'It's easily done.' She had once clicked 'yes' instead of 'no' on her computer and had lost a whole day's work. It could not be got back. 'A whole day's work,' she had said to Bill. 'A whole day wasted.'

Marlene got out her watercolours and took them to the window that had the best view. In the fading afternoon light, she painted a landscape. She took great care over it but later she overheard Travis saying to Bill that the pale green-grey blur in the distance could be land or water, he couldn't tell. 'When she looks at it later,' he said, 'will she know which it is?'

There was a cupboard full of games, and Lizzy and her parents spent a morning playing Twister, while Sue, who did not want to join in, went with Travis to a nearby market.

'What have you got there?' said Bill to Travis when they returned. 'A violin?'

It was a lovely-looking thing he held, like a violin, the glossy wood decorated with black rosemaling and inlaid with mother of pearl, or bone, and at the end of it, carved into the scroll, a head – an animal or a woman, it was hard to tell from a distance.

'Do you know the local story,' said Travis, sitting down and beginning to saw at the strings of his new instrument, 'of Little Freddy with the Fiddle? When he played, everyone started dancing and couldn't stop.'

'You won't get anyone dancing to that racket,' said Bill.

'The man who sold me this said that to become a good fiddler, you must ask the *Fossegrimen* to help you, and he will, for a price.'

'Who's the *Fossegrimen*?'

'A water-dwelling, fiddle-playing spirit.'

'Ah,' said Bill, returning his attention to the Twister board. 'Well, good luck with that.'

The following morning, Travis was the first to get up and by the time everyone else was awake he had already gone out.

'Where's he gone?' asked Sue. 'Why has he gone without me?'

'Never mind,' said Marlene brightly. 'We'll have a day out together, just the family.'

Sue looked at Bill and said nothing, but she sulked all the way round the cider factory and picked a fight with Marlene when Marlene said, 'We'll be going home tomorrow.' No, said Sue, she did not want to go, she did not want to go back to Bill's house, and she harangued her mother throughout the cider tasting.

When they returned to the cabin in the evening, they found Travis there, playing his fiddle. Perhaps, thought Marlene, the cider she had drunk at the factory was affecting her judgement, but his playing seemed quite expert now. The ancient folk music tugged at her heart and, it seemed, at her feet because she did a quick dance in the doorway. Sue, delighted by the sight of him, started laughing and clapping. 'They play the fiddle,' said Travis, 'when they lead a bride to church.'

Bill said to him, 'You've been practising. Good for you.'

They put Lizzy to bed, while Travis continued to play, and then Bill shared out the cider they'd brought back and they sat around drinking and tapping their feet. Marlene fell asleep. When she woke up, it was dark and she was alone.

She found Bill asleep in his clothes in the master bedroom. Lizzy was where they'd left her, in her own bed, but Sue's bed was empty. She woke Bill up. She said, 'I'm getting too old to drink like that. Where's Sue?' And as she spoke, she heard the music. It was coming from outside the house. She turned around and left the bedroom, hurrying out into the night. While Bill blinked in the darkness, Marlene followed the sound of the fiddle music that was floating through the cold night air, pursuing it down a path behind the house. She was running – she could not have said for how long she had been running – when she came to a sudden stop at the sight of Sue dancing at the water's edge while Travis sat beneath an apple tree playing his fiddle. Marlene opened her mouth, but nothing came out, or nothing sufficient to make Sue turn around and look at her mother before jumping into the water. She went under. Marlene shouted, 'Sue!' and ran to the edge, but there wasn't an edge – she stood where the edge should have been and saw that what had surely been water was a field. She stepped onto the surface of it, staring at it, at the place into which she had just seen her daughter leap, staring at the grassed-over earth at her feet. *But it was water*, she thought. She knew it was water. She had seen it. *Wasn't it water?*

She turned to Travis. 'Where is she?'

'Who?' said Travis.

'Sue, where's Sue? Where did she go?'

'You all went to sleep.'

'I saw her jump into the water.'

'What water?' said Travis.

'Where's Sue?' she said again, but the sounds were too soft, the 'wh' and the vowels just exhaled air and the 's' just a hiss like something punctured, and the ground was hard and cold, and Travis was still playing.

The Stone Dead

'THIS GHOST,' SAID Marcus, scratching at the paper with the sharp point of his pencil crayon, 'is green, and he shoots ectoplasm, and his name is Slimo.'

Lesley lifted her own pencil crayon from the intricate labyrinth of her anti-stress colouring book and looked at what her son had drawn, the vivid green scribbled over the outline of his ghost. 'He looks terrifying!' she said.

'And when you look at him,' said Marcus, 'he goes invisible.'

Lesley looked at her watch. 'You can show your drawing to Grandma,' she said. 'She'll be here in five minutes.'

I'll come at one, her mother had said. She always came at one o'clock – it was her time. And she was always precisely on time, on the dot of one. Lesley sometimes wondered if her mother sat outside in the car, or even stood on the doorstep, until the clock struck the hour. She never had to apologise for arriving late, nor looked as if she had rushed.

Lesley went to the window and looked out, but her mother was not in sight. She said to Marcus, 'I'll go and put the kettle on.'

'Can I have a biscuit?' asked Marcus.

'We'll have biscuits when Grandma arrives,' said Lesley.

Lesley was in the kitchen, waiting for the kettle to come to the boil, when the grandfather clock in the hallway struck one. Whatever the hour, the clock chimed once; whether it was one o'clock or midnight, the clock chimed once, and Lesley had begun to associate that single chime with her mother's arrival, so that throughout the day, and every day, when she heard the clock strike one, a little part of her panicked, whether her mother was due or not.

Lesley heard the knock at the door, and when she stepped into the hallway, there was her mother, visible through the glass, as if summoned by the chiming of the clock.

The clock was an heirloom. As a child, Lesley had been afraid of it. Its chiming had made her think of the farmer's wife chasing after the blind mice with her chopper, two different nursery rhymes getting mixed up – she had got confused. And how silly, anyway, she thought, to be afraid of a clock.

'*This* ghost,' said Marcus, appearing beside her, holding up his drawing, 'doesn't have any friends.'

'Well,' said Lesley, 'maybe *we* could be his friends.'

'No,' said Marcus. 'He's not very nice. And he doesn't like us.'

Lesley opened the door and said, 'Come in, Mum.'

'This place is impossible to get to,' said her mother.

'Obviously not *impossible*,' said Lesley, as her mother came in.

Lesley began to close the door, but her mother stopped

her, drawing her attention to the state of the house's exterior. 'Your paintwork's looking tired,' she said. 'I'm having all mine done by a man from the village. He's doing a fairly acceptable job, although he can be lazy; I have to keep an eye on him.'

Her mother's visits always began with a litany of criticisms: the front garden needed weeding; the windows needed washing; Marcus's bike was on the path, in the way. 'And did you have to choose *such* a poky little house?' she asked.

'Can't you ever just be happy?' said Lesley. 'You wanted me to leave Tom, and now I have. You wanted me to move closer to you, and now I have.'

'I wanted you closer than this,' said her mother, following Lesley into the kitchen. 'I thought you were going to live in Sleights.'

'I'm a ten-minute drive from you,' said Lesley. 'That's nothing at all.'

'It's not nothing,' said her mother. 'I seem to be forever on that road, on my way to visit you.'

'Well, you're here now,' said Lesley. 'Shall we have a cup of tea?' She fetched the cups and saucers out of the kitchen cupboard. Her mother would not drink from a mug.

'And biscuits,' said Marcus, who had appeared very suddenly at Lesley's hip.

'Are you going to show Grandma your drawings, Marcus?' asked Lesley.

'Come on, Grandma,' said Marcus, leading his grandmother into the living room. When Lesley went to look, Marcus was saying, 'It doesn't actually have eyes, just black holes that go on for ever and ever and ever.'

The water in the teacups clouded, darkened. Lesley spooned the teabags out and added milk, not too much. She carried the tea and biscuits into the living room, where Marcus was saying, '*This* ghost' – he pointed to a thickly pencilled outline right at the edge of the paper – 'is afraid of all the other ghosts.' Lesley put the tray down on the table, and Marcus reached for the biscuits.

'He watches too much television,' said Lesley's mother.

Maybe he did, but Lesley did not think that was where all these ghosts came from. Ideas just got into his head, like how he used to think that when people died they turned to stone. Where they had lived with Tom, there was a war memorial, whose stone soldiers looked cornered, and Marcus always touched them as he passed. He had seen, in towns and cities, the stone statues of people who had died there. And he saw them in graveyards, the stone dead: men, women, children, dogs. Sometimes, the stone figures were broken, which meant that the ghosts could get out, said Marcus; they did not want to be trapped inside. Lesley sometimes found herself looking at the world the way he did, forgetting for a moment that this was not the way things were.

'He's just got an imagination,' said Lesley.

'He's got *too much* imagination,' said her mother, as if it were a bad thing, like having too many biscuits, like it might make some part of you rot. 'What's this?' she asked, picking up Lesley's colouring book.

'It's a colouring book for grown-ups,' said Lesley.

'What's the point of that?' said her mother.

'It's anti-stress,' said Lesley. 'It's rather nice. It makes me feel like a child again.'

'But you were a miserable child,' said her mother, closing the colouring book and putting it aside. 'What have you been up to?' she said to Marcus. 'I hope you haven't been inside all day. That's not healthy for a boy.'

'We were waiting for you, Mum,' said Lesley. 'I thought we could take some sandwiches down to the beach.'

'In this weather?' said her mother, eyeing the agitation of the bare trees through the cold window.

'We don't have to,' said Lesley.

'No, no,' said her mother, 'if that's what you want to do, that's what we'll do. Though I won't be able to walk on the sand in my heels. I'll have to wear my driving shoes. They'll be ruined.'

Lesley packed up the sandwiches that she had made. Again she said, 'We don't *have* to take these to the beach,' but her mother said, 'No, no, we'll do it your way.'

The three of them went down the steps to the beach, and her mother complained about the distance, and the wetness of the steps, and the damp sand, the damp rocks.

Marcus ran on ahead, this playground vast while the tide was out, and it would not come in until after dark. Every now and then, he stopped to inspect something amongst the rocks, and when he lifted something up, Lesley said to her mother, 'He's found something.'

'Nothing dead, I hope,' said her mother.

Lesley called Marcus over to them. He showed them his grey stone, which he said might have a fossil inside. 'It might have been trapped inside the rock for millions of years.'

'You can put it with the one I gave you for your birthday,' said his grandmother.

'Right,' said his mother, 'sandwich time.'

Marcus put his stone down to take a sandwich from his mother.

'You can have a little fossil collection,' said his grandmother.

'I broke your fossil,' said Marcus.

'You broke it?' said his grandmother. 'Well that was very careless of you. Do you know how old that ammonite was? More than a hundred million years old.'

'It wasn't an accident,' said Marcus. 'I smashed it with a hammer, to let the ghost out.'

Lesley avoided meeting her mother's eye. She said to Marcus, 'At least the ghost will be happy now, won't it? Eat your sandwich.'

'No,' said Marcus. 'It's not happy. It doesn't want to be a ghost. But it did want to get out. The ghosts always want to get out.'

'Eat your sandwich,' said Lesley.

'I'll never give you anything nice again,' said his grandmother.

They ate their sandwiches standing up, huddled into themselves.

They walked along the windswept front and through the town, in whose shops Lesley's mother always seemed to be hunting for something quite precise. She inspected teacups whose pattern was right but whose size was wrong, and side plates whose size was right but whose pattern was wrong. After a couple of hours, Marcus began to complain, until his grandmother shut him up.

They had tea in a cafe. When the waitress came for the

crusts of Marcus's mini pizza, she asked if they would like dessert, and his grandmother said, 'No. No dessert.'

As they left the cafe, Lesley looked up at the darkening sky and said, 'The tide will be turning.'

They made their way back to the house beneath the threat of rain. Lesley and Marcus came into the hallway like people glad to be out of a storm, though it had not yet started. Lesley's mother, who remained on the doorstep, said, 'I'll go now.'

'You don't have to go just yet,' said Lesley. 'Will you have a cup of tea first?'

'No,' said her mother. 'With any luck, I'll make it home before the rain comes.'

'Are you angry, Grandma?' asked Marcus. 'Are you angry because of the fossil?' But she did not reply.

Lesley, unbuttoning her coat, unzipping her boots, asked, 'Are your shoes all right, Mum?'

'They're damp,' said her mother.

'Oh dear,' said Lesley.

'The wet sand has got into them.'

'You'd be welcome to borrow something,' said Lesley.

'Your feet are too small,' said her mother.

Seeing that Marcus was struggling with the zip of his anorak, Lesley bent down to help him. 'Grandma's going now,' she said. 'Say goodbye.'

'Goodbye, Grandma,' said Marcus. 'See you soon.'

The heavens were opening and Lesley said, 'Look at that rain. You can't drive in that, Mum. You don't want to be driving on wet roads.'

'You don't want me spending the night here,' said her mother, 'do you?'

'Will you call?' said Lesley. It was routine for her mother to let Lesley know when she was safely home.

'Yes,' said her mother. 'I'll call.'

'Time to get ready for bed,' said Lesley, steering Marcus into his bedroom. She closed the curtains against the darkness outside.

'I don't want to sleep downstairs,' he said.

'Well,' said Lesley, 'we *have* to sleep downstairs; there's *only* downstairs now. Arms up.' She helped him out of his top.

'I liked our old house better,' said Marcus.

'Yes,' said Lesley. 'Me too. But it's nice being by the sea, isn't it? It's nice living closer to Grandma and Grandpa, isn't it?'

They were quiet for a moment, while outside, the rain continued to fall.

'I don't think Grandma likes me,' said Marcus.

'Of course she does,' said Lesley, holding her son's pyjama trousers for him to step into. 'She comes to see you, doesn't she?'

'She comes,' agreed Marcus, 'but I don't think she likes me.'

'She's upset,' said Lesley, 'because you broke her fossil.'

Marcus climbed into bed. 'Will you stay with me?' he asked.

'I'll stay until you fall asleep,' said Lesley. She lay down with him and read a story, but had to stop because it frightened him. She dimmed the lamp and sang softly until she fell asleep beside him.

◊

The telephone was ringing in the hallway. That's what had woken her. By the dimmed lamplight, she left her son's bed and picked her way across his room, placing her feet carefully between his strewn toys. When she opened the bedroom door, the hallway light that flooded in was painfully bright. She pulled the door to behind her and picked up the phone.

'Lesley,' said her stepfather, 'is Ruth sleeping there?'

'No,' said Lesley. 'Mum left after tea.' The grandfather clock behind her chimed and she turned and saw how late it was. 'She should have been home hours ago.'

'I'm going to drive over,' said her stepfather, 'in case she's broken down somewhere.'

Lesley turned her head towards the front door. Had she heard something? The porch light was on, but she could not see anyone through the glass, on the doorstep. With the phone still pressed against her ear, she went to the door and opened it, but there was nobody there. She looked out at the turbulent night, trying not to think about her mother's car crumpled in a ditch with the doors wedged shut, or shunted under a lorry, her mother dead on impact, or not quite dead but trapped.

'I'll stay near the phone,' she said to her stepfather. There was a tremble in her voice. She felt unsteady. 'Do you think I should call the hospital?' The hairs on her bare forearms were standing on end. She shut the door again, and locked it. As she moved back down the hallway, with her stepfather's voice in her ear, it took her a moment to notice her son, wide awake and standing in his bedroom doorway.

'This ghost can't ever be happy,' said Marcus, and Lesley looked for the drawing in his hands, but his hands were empty. He reached out, to hold on to her, holding on to her clothes, looking towards the front door, in through which had come all the cold air that Lesley could feel at her back, cold air in which the chiming of the grandfather clock still seemed to vibrate.

Ooderwald

THE DOG IS fussing to be let out. 'Not yet,' says Carrie, though she doesn't know if it understands. It knows words like 'walk' and 'fetch', the words of things it likes, and 'no', which it hears a lot.

First, she wants coffee. There is a seemingly bottomless tub of mild blend instant coffee powder in Teresa's kitchen cupboard. Carrie takes a teaspoonful and returns the jar to the cupboard. 'I just have to finish intransitives,' she tells the dog. 'Then we'll go.'

She always wanted a red setter; she even named it, as if that might make it real, but her dad still said no, there wasn't room in their flat. She wanted a horse as well. Now Carrie is old enough to decide for herself but her house share does not allow pets, and there is not much room there either. But this is Teresa's own house, and there is plenty of space. The huge house is detached, with private land on every side. As well as the red setter, Teresa could probably have a horse or two if she wanted.

Teresa worries about burglars, which is why she asked Carrie to house-sit, and why she has told her to keep everything locked even when she's in – all the doors, including the patio doors, and the windows. 'And no parties!' she said, which was a joke.

Teresa would have been home by now, after two weeks of luxury cruising; it was supposed to be a dream holiday but now she's stuck there. She and thousands of others are confined to their cabins; they've been there for weeks and it's not over yet.

So Carrie has stayed on. She is in no hurry to leave. In the house share, her bedroom is just a box room, and nothing is ever clean. Here, she has all these big rooms to herself, and nobody's mess but her own. It's a proper grown-up's house, the kind of house Carrie would like for herself. Teresa's bedroom looks like something out of a Sunday supplement. She has furniture from the Far East, and her wallpaper comes from Farrow & Ball; the en suite bathroom is painted in Elephant's Breath. There is a king-size bed just for Teresa, and a carpet so thick that when Carrie steps on it, she sinks in.

Carrie sleeps in the guest room, which has pea-green walls and matching bedding and a seascape the width of the headboard above which it hangs. She's been having weird dreams, so vivid that when she wakes, they still seem real.

She carries her full coffee mug through the living room, trying not to spoil Teresa's new cream carpet, squatting to soak up drips with a tissue from her cardigan pocket. She works at a laptop at the dining table, and tries not to work while she eats or eat while she works, but frequently finds herself snacking.

There are three more modules in the unit, and five more units in the grammar course. She must learn her own language – the parts she has forgotten, or perhaps has never known – before she can teach it. She had thought she understood the difference between transitive and intransitive verbs, the difference between *She wakes him* and *She wakes.* But she's become confused, and posted a question on the forum last night. *The course*, she wrote, *says, 'He smoked' is transitive because 'a cigarette' is implied. It also says 'I lost' is intransitive, but surely that too has an implied object (as in 'I lost the game'), making it transitive?* The deeper she gets into grammar, the less she finds she knows.

Overnight, a fellow student has posted a reply, which Carrie reads while she drinks her coffee. *'I lost' could mean many things*, the student has written. *You might have lost a game of tennis, or on the way home you might have lost your keys or your money or other things. So it is open ended. I hope that made sense.*

Hi! writes Carrie. *Thanks for your reply. But if I lost my keys on the way home, I'd come home and say 'I lost my keys' – it would make no sense to come in and say 'I lost' if I mean my keys.* Still far from clear, she posts her response and clicks on the jobs page.

There are teaching opportunities across Europe and Asia. 'The world's your oyster,' said her dad, who had moved abroad himself, having found his dream property.

Carrie searches through the job ads, imagining herself in these places, hundreds or thousands of miles away. She has been to Japan. In Tokyo, she encountered a young woman in charge of a group of children with special needs, who had made cakes and were selling them from a stall to passersby. Carrie stopped and looked at what they had, and bought some marble cake. She has always remembered their smiles, the pleasure of the exchange, and how good the cake tasted. She remembers a childhood stall of her own. She and a friend had placed a table on the pavement and filled it with brooches they had made from glossy green leaves from the garden hedge, with a twig poked through at the top and bottom for the pin – the brooches looked like sails filled by the wind. She and her friend made dozens of them and displayed them on their table to sell for 1p each. They stood there all morning, smiling as people passed by. She still remembers the one man – a foreign student from the university, smart in a suit in the heat of summer – who stopped to see what they were selling; she remembers his serious appraisal of their brooches, his appreciation of their good value, his careful choosing, his penny and his big smile.

It would be possible to work from home, from her bedroom, to teach online, across time zones, seeing her students on her laptop screen, the same way she's been seeing her dad recently.

She begins the next module, taking notes, trying to understand. Meanwhile, she haunts the forum, hoping for answers. The dog is waiting, alert, in the doorway. Eventually, closing her laptop, pushing back her chair, Carrie says, 'All right, let's go out.'

There is a full moon in the mid-morning sky. The dog trots along, sniffing at the world. On the riverbank, Carrie unclips its lead and it scampers away. On the far side of the river, she can see Teresa's next-door neighbour Peter, who knows Carrie by now, who always asks, from a safe distance, how she's coping and if she's heard from Teresa;

and ever since Carrie mentioned her dad, Peter always asks after him too. 'His own vineyard,' he said when Carrie told him about her dad's new life in France, 'imagine that.'

Vineyard might be a bit of a stretch, but he grows his own grapes and has been making some wine. They'd been Zooming, she said, or at least they'd tried but the connection was poor and kept dropping out. The screen kept freezing, freeze-framing her dad's confused face.

The neighbour is too far away today for a conversation; they wave to one another from afar, and when he has walked on, Carrie calls to the dog. It has gone out of sight and is hard to fetch back; it will have found a good scent, which might lead to a hole, a burrow.

It comes, in the end, for a biscuit. They go back to the house, where Carrie warms some pea soup. She made too much and has been eating it for days. It is comfort food though: she eats it on the sofa, wrapped in a blanket, and thinks of all the other things she wants. While her window for making changes is still open, she adds everything to her Tesco order and ends up with enough to feed a family.

At bedtime, the dog follows Carrie upstairs to the guest room and sits in the doorway to watch her undress. It will migrate to the master bedroom while she sleeps; in the morning, she will find it sitting at the foot of Teresa's bed, like the dog Hachikō whose statue outside Tokyo's Shibuya Station marks the spot where, in the years after his master's death, Hachikō still waited for him to come home.

Carrie is woken from her deep sleep by the sound of the

telephone ringing downstairs. She gets up, wondering if it might be Teresa, or something to do with her dad.

In the hallway, barefoot on the marble tiles, she lifts the receiver and says, 'Hello?'

There's a delay, and then a voice says, in a foreign accent, 'I want to send a fax.'

Carrie says, 'I think you have the wrong number.' She waits for a response, which doesn't come. She replaces the phone and goes back to bed, watched by the dog.

Sometime later, she wakes again, hearing the ringing of the phone. It is still dark.

The voice at the other end is insistent: 'I want to send a fax.'

'It's the middle of the night,' says Carrie. 'This is just a phone, in someone's house.' She hangs up. She thinks about unplugging it, but worries about people trying to reach her, or people wanting to reach Teresa, who has a phone on the cruise ship but whose signal is intermittent.

She lies awake for an hour or more, and wonders about getting up, but instead falls asleep. She dreams she is meant to be at some function and is in danger of being late; she ought to get going, but first she needs shoes. She's in the middle of nowhere though, in a place called Ooderwald, and even when she finds the visitor centre she's unable to find any shoes. It gets later and later, until she's really up against it. Either she will have to go barefoot, and be late in any case, or she will have to phone and explain why she can't be there. Or, she thinks, maybe this is just a dream; she could stop worrying about it and have a glass of wine in the cafe. She has it in her hand, has the glass to her lips, and can taste the red wine as she wakes.

◊

While Carrie eats her breakfast, the dog sits nearby. Carrie tells it the plan for the day, and discusses points of grammar, and it listens with its head cocked. In addition to verbs, Carrie has been struggling through nouns, including abstract nouns, which, according to her coursework, are things that cannot be experienced with the five senses and which cannot affect us physically. 'But,' she says to the dog, 'what about love? Love is an abstract noun, but it can affect us physically.' Apparently electricity is a concrete noun because you can see its effect. 'But you can see the effect of love as well,' she tells the dog, 'so that doesn't make sense.' The dog looks worried. Carrie takes its photograph with her phone and sends it to Teresa, adding *Bessie misses you*. The dog is also pining for buttered toast. It watches Carrie eating, saliva dripping from its gums; it watches as she eats the final corner and puts her empty plate in the sink.

On the forum, Carrie finds a reply, from a different student, who says, *To see if a verb has an object, you have to ask yourself: 'What have I lost?' The answer is: 'I don't know.' There is no object, so the verb is intransitive.*

Carrie frowns at the screen. This scenario is becoming stranger. She takes a sip of coffee and puts her fingers to the keys. *Hi!* she writes. *But could anyone ever say 'I lost' without meaning they lost something, and without knowing what they lost?*

This discussion, this focus on intransitives, seems to be taking her down a rabbit hole. Despite being snagged on this point, she is continuing to work her way through the course, but there's a possibility – like the time she tried caving, with a compass that let her down – that she will at some point wish to quit, to turn back, to not have started in the first place.

She never realised how many tenses there were. She has been using this language all her life, and yet somehow she was never aware of the existence of the past continuous, the present perfect simple, the future perfect continuous, and multiple conditionals: she would have thought there was only one conditional tense, but now she finds that there is a first and a second. The second conditional is used for imagining unlikely situations. She recognises it when she sees it, and has of course used it herself: *If I won a lot of money, I would buy a big house in the country.* There is a zero conditional, and a third conditional, but she can't imagine what that would be.

The dog is whining to be let out. When Carrie reaches the end of the module, she walks the dog down to the river and unclips its lead. The wind is fierce, and there are needles of rain in the air, but Peter is still out walking; they meet at the weir and have to raise their voices above its noise. She tells him Teresa is still confined to the cruise ship, 'and going stir-crazy.'

'I bet,' says Peter. 'And your dad was self-isolating, wasn't he? How's he doing?'

'He was fine,' says Carrie, 'when I last spoke to him.' She tried calling him last night, but he didn't pick up – which might mean he's out of self-isolation and out and about again. Her dad likes walking; he walks for miles every day if he can. Otherwise, he has told her, he gets restless legs in bed. She gets that too – she knows the feeling of lying in bed, on the edge of sleep, with that unbearable urge in her legs. She thinks it might be some kind of deficiency.

She says to Peter, 'How are you sleeping?'

'Oh,' he says, 'you know.' She does know. He sleeps badly, and often spends the small hours doing puzzles.

She wants to tell someone about her dream. Standing in the cold and the roar of the weir with this neighbour of a friend of a friend, she says to him, 'I had the strangest dream.' She tells him about being stuck in Ooderwald, and trying to buy shoes in a visitor centre, and there being, for some reason, a marching band. Her dream goes on and on, seemingly edgeless.

He has stepped away.

'It still seems so real,' she says.

'I'd better be getting back,' says Peter, moving on, turning once to say, 'Take care,' before heading home.

She can't see the dog. She calls to it. She tries whistling, but what noise she manages is lost to the wind. She doesn't have any biscuits, and knows she'll just have to keep calling and calling until it comes.

When she finally gets the dog back to Teresa's house, she googles Ooderwald. She wondered in her dream if it was German, and there is an Oderwald in Lower Saxony, but no Ooderwald; it doesn't seem to exist. It sounds like a strange, scary forest in a children's book.

She wants to call her dad, but he might be having his lunch and she doesn't want to disturb him. She eats some pea soup and then phones, but he doesn't pick up. When he first moved abroad, he told her there was a spare room, so she could visit. She promised she would, when she could take the time off work. It was the kind of job that ate up all her hours; she never knew where the days went. Her dad always reminds her that she's welcome any time, that she can stay for as long as she likes. She always says she will. He tells her there are the most amazing views.

Now she's lost that job, so she's started this course. When she completes it, she can start working again. She checks the forum; there are no new replies. But, she tells the dog as she presses on through the next module, she knows what the third conditional is now: it refers to the past and can be used to express regrets, 'Like, *If I had won a lot of money, I would have bought a big house in the country.* Or, *If I had had time, I would have—*' She pauses, listening. She shuts her laptop, not sorry to be interrupted by the arrival of the Tesco van.

The delivery man unloads her crates at the kitchen door, making small talk while Carrie lifts her groceries onto the counter. The delivery man, stowing the empty crates, says he's looking forward to the end of the day. 'Have you got plans?' he asks, nodding to the wine she's unpacking.

'Not really,' she says, lining up the bottles.

She inspects the substitutions and puts away the refrigerated and frozen food, then cuts into the marble cake she's ordered. It tastes heavily of vanilla. She drifts back through to the living room, switches on the TV and loses the afternoon to repeats. Towards the end of a murder mystery, she falls asleep, and by the time she wakes again it's dark.

She doesn't feel like cooking, and isn't very hungry

anyway. She eats more marble cake and drinks some wine while she watches an episode of a series she's not really following. She takes a picture of the wine – her solitary glass and the rest of the bottle – types *Wish you were here*, and sends it to Teresa. She lets the dog into the garden and waits at the French windows, gazing out at the dark lawn, the black beds and borders. She imagines her dad, sitting on his patio or balcony with a glass of his own wine, looking out over the grapevines that Carrie has not been to see. He sometimes talks about coming home, about selling his house, his land.

As the dog comes running out of the darkness and into the house, Carrie wonders about calling her dad but there's the time difference between them. She pours herself another glass of red, dials his number and leaves a rambling message that is cut off by the beep.

During the night, the phone rings. Carrie, emerging from her sleep, has a feeling it has been ringing for a while. Her head feels thick and heavy. Leaving her warm bed, she shuffles through the dark house and down to the cold hallway, where she puts the receiver to her ear and says, 'Hello?' Even before she has finished speaking, she hears the noise of a fax machine trying to send. She hangs up and goes back to bed.

In what is left of the night, she has a feverish dream, but struggles to remember it when she wakes.

With an ache in her brain, she checks her phone. There is no message from her dad, no missed call.

Downstairs, she drinks a cup of coffee, and then another one, but still feels half asleep. She regrets the wine. If she hadn't drunk so much last night, she would not have woken up with a headache this morning.

It's not as if she and her dad speak every day, or on regular days – sometimes they don't speak for weeks – but he always returns her calls. She tries his landline again, and then his mobile, and listens as it rings. If he still lived in the family home, she would call the neighbours and ask them to pop round, to check on him, but she doesn't know who his neighbours are now, or how she would contact them.

She's going to be late. She puts on her walking boots, stashes a handful of dog biscuits in her coat pocket and clips the dog's lead to its collar. When they get outside, the dog pulls towards the river, but Carrie walks it in the other direction, through the industrial estate, and along the side of the road for miles. She knows it wants to be off the lead but she can't allow it here, with all this traffic, and its tendency to run away.

The wind is against her all the way to the care home, which is further away from Teresa's house than Carrie had anticipated. She hates being late, and yet she so often is. Her grandma is brought to the designated window and they talk on the phone, looking at one another through the glass, 'Like convicts,' says her grandma.

People have always said that the two of them look alike. She looks at her grandma in the frame of the window, and it's like looking at an image of herself, but distant in time. 'I'm sorry I've not been for a while,' says Carrie. The wind snatches at her words and Carrie puts up her hood. Her grandma, inside the heavily heated home, with her hair carefully set, is in a different climate altogether. 'Have you spoken to Dad recently?' asks Carrie.

Her grandma holds the phone awkwardly, like a walkie-talkie. 'I'm expecting him to call anytime,' she says. 'The last time we spoke he wasn't sleeping too well. Are you sleeping?'

Carrie says she is. She tells her grandma about Ooderwald, and needing to be somewhere urgently, and realising, just as she woke, that it was only a dream.

'They've got curfews there, haven't they?' says her grandma, and Carrie thinks she means Ooderwald, before realising she's talking about the overnight curfews in France.

'We had curfews during the war,' says her grandma. 'And blackout – you've to cover up your doors and windows so the bombs don't drop on you.' There is an intermittent loss of connection, gaps between which Carrie can hear her grandma still talking about the blackout, and then, 'The blood,' says her grandma, 'can't get up to the brain.' Her angina has narrowed her arteries. Her blackouts, she says, are a safety mechanism; the body is forced to the ground, so the blood can flow again.

Carrie's familiar with all of this; her dad has the same condition.

'He'll be coming out of isolation soon,' says her grandma, 'won't he?'

'He might be out already,' says Carrie. It's a little while since they spoke, but at that point he said he was feeling all right.

The dog is pulling on its lead, and her grandma says, 'Someone wants to get going.'

It's lunchtime in the nursing home anyway. Carrie can see people being wheeled away. 'I'll come again soon,' she says, waving through the window, not wanting to be the first to hang up. It doesn't feel so different from talking to her dad through a screen across hundreds of miles.

Tomorrow, she will walk to the cemetery, which is in this same direction but a bit further out. Her mum has a memorial plaque that Carrie will talk to. Her mum's not there; she was scattered in the Lakes but Carrie can't get up there. She will tell her mum she's missed, and she will tell her, *I'm retraining; I'm going to teach, like you and Dad*. It's strange to think of herself stepping into her parents' shoes, though in truth she would expect it to feel stranger than it does. *By the way,* she'll add, *Dad sends his love.*

She walks the dog back to the house, where she makes herself a bowl of pea soup. She thinks about fog, about her dad saying *It's a pea-souper out there*; and she thinks about pease pudding, wondering what that is; she doubts she'd want it, hot or cold or nine days old.

When she has eaten, she sits down at the dining table and opens her laptop. Her face, reflected in the black screen, looks tired. She wakes her laptop up; it displays on its screen a picture of a tiny island somewhere. Every morning it shows her a view and asks her *Like what you see?*, like someone sending a postcard saying *Wish you were here?*

She checks the forum, but there are no new replies. She spends the afternoon working through the last of her grammar modules, at the end of which is a page that says *Congratulations!* Wanting to tell someone, to mark this completion, she takes a picture of the screen and sends it to Teresa.

The dog is there, waiting to be fed. While the dog eats, Carrie microwaves something for herself, a pasta dish that will go well with wine. She takes her dinner to the sofa, eyeing a missed dribble of spilled coffee on Teresa's cream carpet. Settling down on the sofa, she moves a cushion and discovers an old pea-soup stain. She hopes it won't be a nightmare to get out.

After leaving another message for her dad, she looks online, without really knowing what she's looking for – she wants some authority. She makes a list of numbers and works through them, thinking of the cables running under the sea, the distance her voice must travel, the weight of water pressing down from above. An official puts her on hold, and Carrie doodles faces on scrap paper while she waits. She speaks, in her weak French, to one person after another, and in between one office and the next she gets cut off.

She lets the dog into the vast garden and it disappears into the darkness. Carrie waits in the doorway until she grows cold and tired of calling into the night. Leaving the French windows ajar, she wraps herself in a blanket and sits at her laptop scrolling through the discussions on the forum. She can lose hours here, going further and further back through the queries, some of which remain unanswered.

Her own post has a new response. Someone has written, *My understanding is that the verb is transitive if the subject actively loses something: if you lose your keys, that's your own fault. Whereas the verb is intransitive if the subject suffers a loss: a book that has lost something in translation hasn't actively lost anything, it has suffered a loss, or if your firm has lost a contract, you have suffered a loss.*

All right, thinks Carrie, *I see.* She reads the message through again. *You have suffered a loss.* It is the difference between an active and a passive loss. Something like *I lost my dog* can have two very different meanings. But when she looks online, she finds a dictionary that lists the verb as transitive in phrases like *She lost her son in the war* and *They lost everything in the flood*, as if these kinds of loss were, after all, just like losing your keys, as if the subject were in some way to blame.

She is thinking of going into the garden with a torch, in case the dog is stuck somewhere or has got through a gap in the hedge. It's past bedtime and the dog's absence is making her uneasy. She keeps expecting the phone to ring, and to hear, at the far end, Teresa asking her to put Bessie on, or someone speaking with an accent or in French, or just the crackle of a bad line.

It's really too late to call her dad, but still she dials his number. The red wine is still out on the table, and she readies a glass to drink while the phone rings and rings.

Acknowledgements

I'm eternally grateful to my first readers – my husband, Dan, and my agent and editor, Nicholas Royle – for being so generous with their time and support, for the unfailing quality and helpfulness of their feedback and advice, and for always putting things nicely. I'm also grateful to Jen and Chris Hamilton-Emery and everyone at Salt, with thanks to Chris for this collection's striking cover. It's ten years since Salt first published me and – after five novels, three children's books and now two collections of stories – it continues to be a great pleasure to work with such a fantastic team.

I'd also like to thank the editors and publishers who first invited or commissioned these short stories and gave them their first homes. It's an honour to have been published in such fine magazines, journals and anthologies and by some of my favourite presses.

Thanks too to my son, Arthur, for bringing a wealth of enthusiasm and imagination into my world. And of course, heartfelt gratitude to all my readers, for their time and their interest and for truly lovely responses to my work – that, above all, is what keeps me writing.

Acknowledgements

'Eastmouth' ©2014, originally published in *The Spectral Book of Horror Stories* (Spectral Press)
'May Day' ©2018, originally published in *High Spirits: A Round of Drinking Stories* (Valley Press)
'Summerside' ©2014, originally published in *Shadows & Tall Trees Vol. 6* (Undertow Publications)
'Fidelity' ©2022, original to this collection
'The Voice of the People' ©2017, originally published in *Shadows & Tall Trees Vol. 7* (Undertow Publications)
'Seabound' ©2021, originally published in *Out of the Darkness* (Unsung Stories)
'The Harvestman' ©2015, originally published as a chapbook (Nightjar Press)
'The Papergirl' ©2022, original to this collection
'Winter Closing' ©2013, originally published in *The Longest Night* (Curious Tales)
'Point of Entry' ©2013, originally published in *Crime* (Nottingham Writers' Studio)
'The Sketch' ©2018, originally published in *New Fears 2* (Titan Books)
'A Month of Sundays' ©2014, originally published in *Solstice Shorts* (Arachne Press)
'Broad Moor' ©2019, originally published as a chapbook (Nightjar Press)
'Pieces' ©2015, originally published in *Black Balloon* (Launderette Books)
'The Spite House' ©2014, originally published in *Poor Souls' Light* (Curious Tales)
'The Meantime' ©2015, originally published in *The 2nd Spectral Book of Horror Stories* (Spectral Press)
'Common Ground' ©2022, original to this collection

'Burning the Winter' ©2016, originally published in *Stories* (PowWow Festival of Writing)
'Hardanger' ©2014, originally published in *AM Magazine* (Illustrated London News Limited)
'The Stone Dead' ©2017, originally published in *The Shadow Booth Vol. 1*
'Ooderwald' ©2021, originally published in *Same Same but Different* (Everything with Words)

This book has been typeset by
SALT PUBLISHING LIMITED
using Granjon, a font designed by George W. Jones
for the British branch of the Linotype company in the
United Kingdom. It is manufactured using Holmen
Bulky News 52gsm, a Forest Stewardship Council™
certified paper from the Hallsta Paper Mill in Sweden.
It was printed and bound by Clays Limited in Bungay,
Suffolk, Great Britain.

CROMER
GREAT BRITAIN
MMXXII